BLACK LIBRARY CELEBRATION 2024

After you enjoy the stories in this anthology, we recommend the following titles:

BRUTAL KUNNIN
Mike Brooks

WARBOSS
Mike Brooks

DA BIG DAKKA
Mike Brooks

CREED: ASHES OF CADIA
Jude Reid

DOMINION
Darius Hinks

THE LAST VOLARI
Gary Kloster

UNTAMED REALMS
Various authors

HORUS RISING
Dan Abnett

WARHAMMER™
HORROR

GOTHGHUL HOLLOW
Anna Stephens

THE RESTING PLACES
Various authors

WARHAMMER™
CRIME

BLOODLINES
Chris Wraight

THE KING OF THE SPOIL
Jonathan D Beer

SANCTION & SIN
Various authors

WARHAMMER™ HORROR

WARHAMMER™ CRIME

BLACK LIBRARY CELEBRATION 2024

Mike Brooks, Gary Kloster, Jude Reid,
Chris Thursten & Jonathan D Beer

A BLACK LIBRARY PUBLICATION

'Packin' Heat', 'The Waste, the Worm, and the Witch', 'The Shel'tain Affair', 'Pain Engine' and 'Chains' first published digitally in 2022. This edition published in Great Britain in 2024 by Black Library, Games Workshop Ltd., Willow Road, Nottingham, NG7 2WS, UK.

Represented by: Games Workshop Limited – Irish branch, Unit 3, Lower Liffey Street, Dublin 1, D01 K199, Ireland.

10 9 8 7 6 5 4 3 2 1

Produced by Games Workshop in Nottingham.
Cover illustration by Tazio Bettin.

A CIP record for this book is available from the British Library.

ISBN 13: 978-1-80407-358-2

Printed and bound in the UK.

CONTENTS

PACKIN' HEAT

MIKE BROOKS

What do I do about a problem like Nizkwik?

This had been the question going round Snaggi Littletoof's head for days, but the answer still eluded him. He *should* have been grotboss by now, lauded and celebrated as the greatest gretchin to have ever lived, and leading his own Waaagh! in a glorious crusade against humies, bugeyes, and anyone that wanted to stop him from getting his claws on their stuff. Unfortunately the orks over whom he should be ruling had ignored the will of the gods, and after a particularly traumatic journey through some inter-dimensional portals he'd ended up here, on a world mainly consisting of grass and dust and mountains, and right back down the pecking order in a completely different Waaagh! The TekWaaagh!

And subservient to Nizkwik.

'Oi, Snaggi!' Nizkwik hollered. 'Bring dat oil squig over 'ere!'

Snaggi grimaced, but picked the rotund little creature up

and crossed the floor of the big boss' bunker to place it in the hand of Nizkwik as he sat, eyes crossed with concentration, in front of the big boss' third-favourite slugga.

Nizkwik was another grot. He was the grot's grot. If you took all the grots in the galaxy, ground them down to their component atoms, and then made the single grottiest grot you could from what you had, it would look like Nizkwik. He had everything you'd expect in a grot: the dagger-like nose, the ragged batwing ears, the long clawed fingers, the pale green skin, and the tattered clothing in the colours of the orks he served: yellow and black in this case, since the TekWaaagh! was dominated by Bad Moons. On the face of it, there was nothing to distinguish Nizkwik from the veritable hordes of grots that existed throughout the galaxy.

Snaggi, however, knew better.

Nizkwik was the personal grot of Ufthak Blackhawk: the big boss in charge of this part of the TekWaaagh!, and an ork that was not only massive but utterly fearsome. Snaggi didn't trust Ufthak, not one bit. He was too smart for an ork, too smart by half, with a nasty habit of following facts through to a logical conclusion. An ork that smart was bad news for everyone. Or at least, bad news for Snaggi, which was basically the same thing. After all, how was Snaggi supposed to have another stab at fulfilling his gods-given destiny and becoming grotboss if an ork like Ufthak was hanging around ready to stamp on him? It was zoggin' unfair, is what it was.

Nizkwik was the key, Snaggi was sure. The other grot had somehow managed to inveigle his way into Ufthak's surroundings, and had become if not actively welcome, at least tolerated in the sense that Ufthak yelled at him to do things rather than get lost. In Snaggi's experience, that was as close to an expression of trust as orks got when it came to grots. Nizkwik must have some special understanding of orkish nature in order to manage this, and Snaggi needed it.

However, Nizkwik must also have his own plans, since no grot got close to an ork unless he had to. A grot's natural instinct was to do as little as possible, nick stuff, and throttle anything smaller that annoyed him, while an ork's natural instinct was to make grots do everything for them except fighting. That wasn't to say they didn't make grots fight as well, just that the orks wanted what they considered the most fun for themselves, which meant using grots as living shields for the dull stuff like getting shot at. It was surely one of the gods' greatest jokes, Snaggi had previously reflected, that orks and grots were almost always in close proximity to each other.

Snaggi's preferred place was well away from an ork's eye, either doing something unimportant that no ork bothered to check up on or, preferably, plotting his own ascension to glory while a group of other grots convinced of his genius ran around for him and they all awaited the perfect moment to overthrow their masters. He had decided to make an exception here, simply because he had to find out what Nizkwik was up to. What was his plan? Why did it involve being so close to Ufthak? And how did the deceitful little git manage to never give himself away?

'Dere we go,' Nizkwik said with every indication of happiness, squeezing the oil squig onto the slugga. He worked the weapon's action, ensuring the oil was evenly distributed and the moving parts flowed smoothly past each other, then placed it carefully back. Snaggi watched the whole procedure closely, but saw no sign anything was amiss. The oil was genuine squig oil rather than some corrosive substance, and no miniature explosive had been planted to make the slugga explode if Ufthak fired it. To all appearances, Nizkwik was genuinely servicing the big boss' weapons when Ufthak wasn't even around and telling him to do it.

The fiendish complexity of it! Snaggi considered himself a strategic mastermind, but this long game was currently beyond his comprehension. He would have to stay on his guard, because Nizkwik surely had exactly the same doubts about why Snaggi was here. They were two trampla squigs circling each other – not yet at the stage of snorting and pawing at the ground prior to charging, but definitely eyeing each other up and working out their rival's intentions.

Snaggi was concerned that he was at a disadvantage. Nizkwik had been around the TekWaaagh! longer, so this was essentially his home turf. He knew the important orks and what would enrage them, and he knew the hidden strata of grot society; indeed, he sat somewhere near the top, based simply on his status as 'Ufthak's grot'. If Nizkwik decided that Snaggi was a problem or a threat, then Snaggi was likely to become squig food after he got blamed for nicking Da Boffin's hammer-wrench, or Dok Drozfang's favourite scalpel, even if he'd been nowhere near either ork at the time.

Perhaps, Snaggi thought, it was time to come clean, rather than wait for Nizkwik to start hostilities when he wasn't looking. Nonetheless, this was going to take subtlety.

'So,' he said conspiratorially, sitting down on the floor next to Nizkwik. 'Wot's da plan?'

Nizkwik looked at him, his brow wrinkling in confusion. 'Da plan?'

'Yeah,' Snaggi prompted. 'Ya know. For da boss.' He waggled his eyebrows knowingly.

'For da... Oh. *Ohhh.*' Realisation dawned on Nizkwik's

features, closely followed by suspicion. 'How'd yoo know about da plan?'

Snaggi suppressed a thrill of excitement that his genius insight had, once again, been accurate. 'Well, sort of obvious yoo're gonna have a plan, innit?' he said, then realised how that sounded and hastily back-tracked. 'I mean, not obvious to *everyone,* of course not to *everyone,* but to anuvver grot wot's hangin' around and has da same sort of brain...' He tapped the side of his nose. 'Yoo can trust me. Promise.'

Nizkwik's eyes narrowed. 'Promise?'

'Promise,' Snaggi said, making his own face as open and honest as possible. He didn't mention anything about how trusting him only extended so far as him not instantly revealing that plan to Ufthak, and should in no way be interpreted as trusting him not to, for example, quite literally stab Nizkwik in the back once he'd gleaned every useful scrap of information he could from the other grot.

'Well, alright den!' Nizkwik said with satisfaction. 'Wiv two of us, we can get dis done! Come wiv me!' He got to his feet and trotted out of the bunker without a backward glance. Snaggi hurried up and followed him, grinning as he went, eager not to let this new-found trust expire through tardiness.

Finally, a breakthrough!

Nizkwik led the way with the casual aplomb of someone who had long ago learned which squig pens were too ramshackle to venture near in case the occupants got excited at the sight of a grot and burst loose to try to eat you, which areas of open ground you only ventured into if you wanted to get mashed flat by the speed freeks as they engaged in their near-incessant races, and which piles of junk were prone to explode without warning as a mekboy tested his latest invention. Snaggi kept up, storing all this information away for future use and wondering what exactly they were after. Were they stealing a particularly powerful weapon from a mekboy's workshop to vaporise Ufthak when he returned, in order to then take command of the Waaagh! through force of arms? Were they going to nick experimental gubbinz from a painboy which they would clamp to Ufthak's skull when he was asleep, and somehow control his brain and therefore his behaviour? Were they going to stab someone?

Apparently not. They passed through the riotous core of the camp, through the bustling markets where teef were traded for guns and ammo, fungus beer and fried squig legs, new boots, and armour with only one previous owner who sold it cos he got somefing better, definitely not because he died – ignore da hole in da back of it, dat's just for flexibility so yer arms don't get stuck when yoo're swingin' yer choppa, right?

Then they snuck through where the bulk of the orks camped down, which was in many respects a lot more dangerous. Orks in the markets were busy making or selling wares, or buying and testing those wares. A grot might find himself suddenly used as target practice to test the accuracy of a slugga, but other than getting kicked for being in the way, being victimised by an ork in those surroundings was a relatively rare occurrence: orks only tended to turn on grots when they literally had nothing better to do.

Out where the orks camped, they *didn't* have anything better to do. Any ork who hadn't found an actual enemy to get stuck into was mooching around, waiting either for the nob to decide zog this, they were going out to try to find something to fight; or for the distant sound of dakka to be carried in on the breeze, at which point they would take up their weapons and pile off in that direction as fast as possible.

A pair of grots would make a suitable, if short-lived diversion for any number of the brutes currently kicking their heels.

'Wot are we doin' here?' Snaggi hissed as they weaved their way through the maze of ramshackle huts, crude tents, and rough shelters thrown together from bits of wreckage.

'Gotta get to da uvver side,' Nizkwik said. 'C'mon, dis way!' He picked up his pace, little legs flashing back and forth, and Snaggi had to break into a run to keep up with him.

He thought they'd been discovered when a nearby rumble of ork voices rose into a roar, and he had a sudden mental image of being chased and shot at until the sheer volume of fire overcame even the orks' natural lack of accuracy, but then they crept past the back half of a trukk and he saw a big crowd of orks standing in a circle, far too close for comfort, but all fixated on something in the middle of them.

'Dis is da best way,' Nizkwik whispered, with some satisfaction. 'Sneak past 'em while dey're busy!'

Snaggi paused for a moment in morbid fascination, as the snarling, snorting shape of a smasha squig ran straight at an ork. Instead of scrambling out of the way, the ork charged it with his own head lowered: there was a sickening crunch on impact and then, to Snaggi's shock, the squig toppled sideways with its eyes rolled back and tongue lolling out, while the ork staggered around in a triumphant circle; obviously woozy, but still on his feet.

'Dat's just Mogrot,' Nizkwik said dismissively. 'He won a headbuttin' contest wiv a wall, once.'

Snaggi started to become suspicious when they made it past the last few shelters, and were hurrying across scrubby grass and dusty soil towards the low hills that lay just beyond. However, Nizkwik wasn't reaching for his blasta, and Snaggi couldn't think that the other grot had set up some sort of ambush with any third party. Strange though it might seem, he had to assume there was a genuine purpose to them coming all the way out here. The best thing to do was to be patient and wait for it to become clear.

'Woss goin' on?' he said, grabbing Nizkwik's arm. 'Where're we goin'?'

'Up dere!' Nizkwik said, pointing ahead of them. Halfway up the nearest hillside was a dark hole – a cave? Or, Snaggi thought as he squinted up at it, an entrance. There looked to be stones around it, which suggested that someone had thought it was important enough to prop open and mark.

'Wossat?' he asked.

'I'll show ya!' Nizkwik replied happily, and scurried off again. Snaggi followed him, wondering exactly when the other grot was going to drop his brainless act. Surely at some point soon they would be able to have a conversation about the nature of Nizkwik's plan, and how he intended to seize control?

The climb up the side of the hill was exhausting, but grots were naturally fit and resilient, mainly because any grot that wasn't could expect to be flattened in short order in the hustle and bustle of an ork camp. When they reached the entrance, Snaggi realised that it had caved in only a few feet back from the outside, leaving a pile of rock and earth that blocked access.

'Dis is a speshul place for da skrawniez wot lived 'ere before da Waaagh! came,' Nizkwik said, beaming with glee. 'Dey were sort of Snakebite skrawniez, rode around on dere versions of squigs an' not many of 'em had da usual skrawnie weapons, but some of 'em had da good stuff, like da nobz an' dat. I heard Da Boffin tell da boss dat dere was probably some fancy skrawnie weapons in dis hill, since dey fought really hard to keep us out of it an' pulled da roof down at da end, but da boss said he couldn't be bovvered to go diggin' when dere woz still plenty of skrawniez to scrag out 'ere, and den he hauled Da Boffin off to do somefing else, but I *remembered.*'

Snaggi felt a grin of his own creep across his face. Skrawniez were annoying gits, all flippy and zippy so you thought they weren't going to do anything, then *surprise,* they'd shot you full of their whizzer-discs and you were in seventeen pieces on the floor. Skrawnie weapons were *weird,* but they often hit harder than they looked like they should, *and* – and this was important – they tended to be a lot lighter than ork weapons. That was important: a good shoota weighed as much as a grot. This made stealing a good weapon from an ork almost impossible, which so far as Snaggi was concerned was just another example of the galaxy's shameless conspiracy against him.

Skrawnie weapons, on the other hand... Snaggi reckoned he could lift one, *easy.* If he could lift it then he could shoot it, and if he could shoot it then suddenly the balance of power between him and the orks had shifted.

'So, how do we get in?' he asked eagerly. In answer, Nizkwik pointed to a small, dark hole at about waist height in the tumbled blockage, where a large stone had become wedged over a couple of others as it fell, leaving a gap beneath.

'Froo dere,' Nizkwik said. 'Dat's a start, anyway. Ain't dis *excitin'*?'

'Excitin',' Snaggi muttered, eyeing the hole. 'Yeah.' He thought for a second about how much he would enjoy vaporising or eviscerating any orks that got in his way with the treasures that could lie on the other side of this obstacle, and the sheer power he would feel as a result. His ascension to grotboss would be unquestioned! And of course, once he had his hands on whatever lay inside, there was no reason why Nizkwik should make it out again.

'Yeah!' he said with more enthusiasm, heading for the hole. Snaggi Littletoof had been shoved into worse and smaller places than this before now, and for considerably less potential reward. Now he was doing it on *his* terms.

'Come to Snaggi,' he hissed, clawing his way forward into the darkness.

Darkness. That was the problem.

It was as dark as the inside of a squig, which Snaggi supposed he should have guessed beforehand, but he pressed on and wriggled his way forwards by touch, silently cursing Nizkwik all the way. Why couldn't the git have *told* him they were going underground? Well, there was no way he was going to give the other grot the satisfaction of backing out again and wailing about being unable to see. Claustrophobia was not something you suffered from as a grot, or at least not for long; orks would shove grots into any small space to find out why something was broken or to try to fix it, and if you panicked and came back out without having done the job then the ork would probably feed you to a squig. As a result, the only grots that tended to survive were the ones who had no problem with small spaces, if not actively sought them out as somewhere orks couldn't reach you.

Snaggi froze as a new thought struck him. What if Nizkwik was even now preparing to bring down the unstable rocks? What if he had identified Snaggi as a rival and a threat, and was seeking to either crush him or trap him here? Being comfortable in small spaces was all very well, but that was assuming there was a way out again. It was a cunning plan – Snaggi could tell, because he'd just thought of it – and utterly deniable. Snaggi could just hear Nizkwik's artfully innocent voice now, explaining things to Ufthak: 'I told 'im not to go in, boss, but 'e wouldn't listen!'

Snaggi told himself he was being ridiculous. Nizkwik wouldn't have to explain things to Ufthak, mainly because the big boss wouldn't care enough to ask.

Well, if Snaggi's pride wouldn't let him reverse out, and staying in place and waiting for Nizkwik to collapse the entrance on him wasn't a good idea – which it definitely wasn't – then the only thing for it was to press on as quickly as possible and get out before his treacherous companion could complete his dastardly deed. Snaggi huffed and wriggled, squirmed and crawled, until finally his groping hands found not just a narrow aperture ahead of him surrounded by more rock and earth, but an actual opening too. He pulled himself through eagerly, his little pot belly scraping over the last stone, and flopped onto a hard, flat rock surface: presumably the floor of the cave which had been blocked off. The air was warm in here, far warmer than outside, and smelled sour.

His head came up as he realised that there was light emerging from the hole out of which he'd just exited, and he sat up just in time to see Nizkwik's head appear. The git had a lamp strapped to his forehead!

'Where'd ya get dat?!' Snaggi asked, outraged.

'Dis?' Nizkwik looked up towards his forehead, where Snaggi's finger was pointing. 'Nicked it off a mek ages ago. Fort yoo'd have one. Here ya go!' He pulled a similar lamp-and-strap combination out of his belt pouch and handed it over.

Snaggi took it without a word, his inherent distrust at

Nizkwik not giving it to him at the start not exactly mollified by this act of generosity, more balanced out by a different sort of distrust at it being handed over so casually now. Still, being able to see with both hands free was definitely an advantage.

'Right,' Nizkwik said, emerging fully from the hole. 'Let's get da goods!' He drew his blasta and Snaggi imitated him, partly because he had no intention of letting another grot be armed next to him without having the means to defend himself, and partly because a nasty thought had just occurred to him.

'Nizkwik,' he said. 'Y'know when da skrawniez pulled da tunnel down... Were any of 'em *inside* at da time? Like, trappin' 'emselves inside wiv da loot? Waitin' to slice us into tiny pieces, is wot I'm gettin' at.'

'Dunno!' Nizkwik said cheerily. 'I fort dey all stayed outside an' got stomped by da ladz, but I could be wrong! Now come on!' he said, forging ahead and brandishing his blasta.

Snaggi hesitated for a moment, trapped in an agony of indecision. On the one hand, the sensible thing to do was to back away, squeeze through the hole, quietly return to the camp at a casual saunter, and let Nizkwik get dismembered by whatever terrifying guardian had been left in here. On the *other* hand, Snaggi was damned if he was going to let Nizkwik get any potential glory for himself, let alone any appealingly powerful skrawnie weapons. Being a grot-boss came with responsibilities, damn it, and one of those responsibilities was not letting another grot have anything better than you did.

'Fine,' he muttered, slinking along in Nizkwik's wake. 'Yoo go first.'

The cave tunnel into which they had emerged ran for a

short way further, turning a couple of corners as it did so. As they rounded the first corner Snaggi realised that there was a dim red light from ahead, sufficient to render the tunnel as textured shadow in his vision rather than simple blackness wherever his lamp beam failed to reach.

Then they rounded the second corner, and his trepidatious inner musings about the light's origin disappeared in a wash of awe.

They had emerged into a much wider cavern, the floor of which dropped away from the stone walkway that ran around the edge, and on which they were now standing. Both grots stopped for a moment and stared about them, the beams of their headlamps skittering off into the red-lit gloom. Snaggi's eyes found shaped rock walls into which had been carved fantastically detailed friezes depicting warriors and combat. He shuddered involuntarily as his eyes lit upon the telltale smooth lines and pointed helmets of skrawnie armour, and their slender weapons, distinguishable even when rendered in two-dimensional images. Ranged against them – and dying – were an assortment of foes, many of which Snaggi could recognise from his own heroic adventures around the galaxy in the service of Gork and Mork. There were the heavy-shouldered, pointy-nosed shapes of beakies – real proper beakies like all the boyz said used to show up for fights, not the new-fangled version with flat faces – and their weedy little regular humie mates; the four-armed, many-toothed bugeyes and their various weird beasties; even a few short, thickset shapes with prominent beards which Snaggi took a moment to place.

'Wow,' he said. 'I ain't seen a stunti in *ages.*'

'Dese gits really liked makin' rock look like somefing else, innit?' Nizkwik commented, staring around. 'How bored d'ya have to be to look at a rock an' fink, "Y'know wot dis needs? A picture of me an' all me mates on it!"?'

Snaggi took a tentative step towards the edge, wary both of treacherous footing and the potentially treacherous grot next to him, and looked down. The strange, sour smell he'd already been detecting rose up and smacked him in the nostrils, along with a great rush of heat. Eyes watering, he squinted downwards into the red glow and saw, through heat haze that made the air shiver and shake, a pool of molten rock. Most of the surface was a thick crust of black, but it was shot through with cracks and veins of liquid fire, and as he watched, a portion of it went *glooop* and bubbled upwards, bursting with a wet slowness that revealed a fiery, furiously intense cherry red beneath.

'Urk,' he muttered, backing away hastily. Still, they were here, and there was no other option except to go back, so he began to make his way cautiously along the rock path that ran around the wall to the right.

'Yoo'd fink dere'd be a rail or somefing,' Nizkwik said uneasily, pressed up behind him a little too close for Snaggi's comfort.

'Skrawnie place, innit?' Snaggi pointed out. 'If ya try an' stab 'em, da gits'll jump up an' balance on da blade edge. Dey don't need a rail to stop 'em fallin' anywhere.' Not that rails were a prominent feature in much ork engineering either, but that was less because orks had an innate sense of superb balance, and more because watching other orks fall off things was funny.

They edged forwards, and downwards, because the path was starting to dip. Snaggi was a little unnerved by that, but although it was hard to see in the fire-tinted darkness, there looked to be an opening off into the stone wall on the right well before the path ran on down to the level of the molten rock pool. He began to pick up his pace a little bit, eager to get into a side chamber and away from the source of the sulphurous stink, and realising that once you'd become accustomed to the idea of burning death awaiting you below, the path itself wasn't that narrow. It didn't show any signs of weapons, though.

Another grot – a grot less blessed with intelligence – might have made some comment of that nature to Nizkwik. They might have highlighted how their expectations were not being met, or even uttered dire imprecations for what might happen if this state of affairs did not change. Snaggi, of course, was far too wily to do such a thing. If he was going to engage in vicious, bloody betrayal – no, that was a negative attitude: *when* he was going to engage in vicious, bloody betrayal – he would do so without having given any warning of his intentions beforehand, in order to ensure maximum effectiveness with minimum risk.

'So,' he said brightly. 'Got any idea where we might find da loot?'

'Try dat cave up ahead,' Nizkwik replied excitedly. 'Dat looks like da sort of place ya might find somefing good!'

Snaggi had, of course, already thought just such a thing, only he'd done so in far less pathetic language. He was somewhat taken aback by the lack of any sign of betrayal so far, but Snaggi wasn't going to demand to know Nizkwik's true plans when there was a pool of molten rock so nearby. Let him have his fun, and think Snaggi was still taken in. That just meant that when Nizkwik attempted his own inevitable betrayal, he'd have no idea that Snaggi was ready.

The heat got more intense the lower they went – which just went to show that Mek Zagblutz had been wrong about his claims that heat rose, but what could you expect from an ork? – and Snaggi's skin was starting to feel a little tender by the time the cave entrance loomed up. He ducked into it gratefully and advanced into the darkness, almost as glad to be moving away from the molten rock as he was to be heading towards something that might actually make this journey worthwhile.

And there it was, ahead of them.

The cave led to a chamber, far smaller than the one behind them, but still many times Snaggi's height and a goodly distance from wall to wall. It was illuminated by the faintest light from cut crystals set in sconces, and whoever had carved the walls outside had really let themselves go in here. Coiling plants and leafy vines so realistic that Snaggi almost expected them to sway in a non-existent breeze reached up towards the depiction of a sun that occupied the ceiling, and trailed between archways that contained wondrously detailed statues.

'Argh!'

Nizkwik yelped suddenly, and Snaggi whirled around with his blasta levelled, only to find the other grot on his backside on the floor and chuckling ruefully.

'Gave me a shock, it did,' Nizkwik said, pointing. Snaggi peered, then gave a start of his own: lurking half-hidden behind the carved creepers was a monstrous reptilian shape, so artfully rendered that it looked exactly like a predator waiting to spring.

'Pull yerself togevva,' he snapped, not wishing to admit how startled he'd been. 'Look. *Look!*'

There was a plinth in the middle of the room, the sides of which were decorated with more reptiles: long, sinuous shapes covered with thousands of individually carved scales and with flames erupting from their mouths, and so interwoven that every space between two of them appeared to be occupied by yet another. However, it was not the artwork that had grabbed Snaggi's attention, but what rested on the plinth's flat top.

It was a gun. It was a *skrawnie* gun. It was smooth and largely matt-black, with a cylindrical canister set on the underside just in front of the firing mechanism, and a roughly conical, fire-red barrel, which narrowed to something that looked like a nozzle. It was beautiful and deadly and glorious, and Snaggi wanted to hold it and fire it more than he had ever wanted anything in the galaxy.

'Ooooooh,' Nizkwik said, getting up with his eyes wide. 'Wot d'ya fink it does?'

'Dere's all dese pictures of fingies breathin' fire, an' it's in a cave next to a pool of melty rock,' Snaggi pointed out, 'so I reckon it's one of dere fancy burnas.' He shoved his blasta into his belt and flexed his fingers avariciously as he reached out with both his hands. This wasn't something you just *grabbed.* He wanted to make it a *moment* – something that divided his life between the before, when he didn't have the burna, and after, when he did have the burna and everyone who'd wronged him was going to be *sorry.*

'Snaggi?'

He gritted his teeth in frustration. Nizkwik was definitely going to be first on the sorry list. '*Wot?*'

'Did dat statue just... move?'

Snaggi looked around. The statue in question was of a skrawnie warrior, complete with blank-eyed helm, but in somewhat different armour to what Snaggi had seen before. It was less form-fitted, more obvious plates with soft cloth between, and a cloak of actual fur that looked far too primitive for most skrawniez. This must be a representation of one of the beast snagga-types Nizkwik had mentioned, the backwater skrawniez who lived on this world and were in the process of being exterminated by the TekWaaagh! It was so lifelike that in the dim light, the stone it was carved from almost seemed to possess actual colour.

'Nah,' he said, staring at it. 'It's just yer imagi-*zoggin' 'eck!'*

The skrawnie...

...moved.

It lurched forwards, bringing a long blade up in its left hand. Snaggi made an abortive grab for the burna, then jerked backwards as the blade came down where his wrists had been a moment before. The edge bit into the stone, and the skrawnie took a moment to heave the blade out again, giving Nizkwik a chance to empty his blasta in its direction with an ongoing scream that appeared to be in defiance of the notion of concepts like breathing and airflow.

The wall behind the skrawnie popped and puffed with dust and chips of stone as the slugs struck home, but as Nizkwik's blasta ran dry and his scream finally tailed off, the skrawnie itself remained unhurt. It looked down at itself in apparent disbelief, then its head snapped back up and it finally pulled its sword free again.

'Arrgh! It's a ghost, it's a ghost!' Nizkwik wailed, back-pedalling until he came up against the wall behind him.

'Nah, ya just can't shoot!' Snaggi snarled, hauling his own blasta out of his belt. The skrawnie stepped forwards again, blade swinging menacingly, but Snaggi had seen real skrawnie warriors in action and although this one wasn't a ghost, it was certainly only a pale shadow of its kin. It was slow and clumsy in comparison, and where its first thrust should have spitted him like a roasted squig, he was able to dodge aside from it and fire two shots.

The first one struck the skrawnie in the chest, and the force of the impact stopped it in its tracks. The second took it in the right knee, and blew the joint out in a spray of blood and bone. The skrawnie collapsed with a grunt of pain, and Snaggi put his next shot right between where its eyes presumably were under its helmet.

The shot knocked it onto its back, the strange substance skrawniez used as armour cracked and split, and the parts of the helmet fell away to reveal a face that even Snaggi recognised as old. The hair was white and lank, the cheeks were sunken and lined, the eyes milky and struggling to focus. How long had it been standing here, guarding that weapon, waiting for an intruder or, perhaps, one of its own kind to show up and take it to use in battle?

Snaggi didn't know, and realised he didn't care. The only thing standing between him and his destiny was at the end of his gun, and he was about to–

'Outta da way, Snaggi! I'm gonna toast 'im!'

Snaggi looked around in horror, but sure enough Nizkwik had hauled the burna – *Snaggi's burna!* – off the plinth and was fumbling it around to aim it at the skrawnie.

Snaggi saw red. Absolute fury washed through him, fury mixed with envy at Nizkwik being the first grot to ever get their hands on that beautiful death machine, and also mixed with trepidation, because he *was* standing directly in front of the gun and Nizkwik's finger *was* slipping closer to the firing stud, and Snaggi *wasn't* sure that the other grot was going to have either the ability or inclination to stop it...

'Oh, zog,' Snaggi said, and dived to one side.

On the floor, the skrawnie laughed: a harsh, broken sound flecked with pain and malice. Snaggi had just enough time to wonder what that was about, and then Nizkwik fired the burna and Snaggi's eyeballs fused to the back of his skull.

Or at least, that was what it felt like. The weapon's beam was a lance of acetylene fire, even harsher than normal in this gloom, which scored a line across Snaggi's vision so bright and lingering that for a moment he struggled to tell whether his eyes were open or not. When he began to make out details again, the skrawnie was mostly gone. Its legs were still there, although the upper edges of the remaining fabric were on fire. The lower half of its torso was a blackened ruin, which flaked away into ash round about the chest area, and everything above that was just... gone. Unless you counted the black smear on the floor, or the fine particles that now laced the air.

'*Wow!*' Nizkwik said happily, grinning from ear to ear. 'Dis is *amazing!*'

'Dat's *mine,*' Snaggi growled, but he growled it very quietly, because it was unwise to show aggression in front of a grot who could vaporise you with a twitch of his finger. Then he blinked. 'Er, are me eyes still messed up, or is dat glowin'?'

Lines of cold light had descended from the top of the plinth, and were now spreading across the floor. Snaggi scrambled out of the way of one of them, which ran on and into the wall.

Something above them creaked. Snaggi looked at the now-empty plinth, at the gun in Nizkwik's arms, thought back to the skrawnie laughing in the face of its impending death, and put things together faster than a mekboy on fungus drops.

'Leg it!' he yelled, getting to his feet and bolting for the tunnel that would take them back to the main cavern.

'I'm right behind ya!' Nizkwik said encouragingly as Snaggi shot past him. There was an almost overwhelming urge to turn, to insist that Nizkwik go first and then shoot him in the back, steal the burna and leave him here, but even Snaggi's greed took orders from his self-preservation. He ran on as fast as he could, relieved to hear Nizkwik's feet pattering on the stone behind him. At least the git was bringing himself along so Snaggi could slit his throat and get the weapon off him later.

He slowed and cut hard left at the main cavern, pounding up the rock path as fast as his feet could carry him. The cold light was keeping pace, spreading out and running in angular lines through the carved friezes, casting new shadows over the sculpted figures as it went. Snaggi yelped in terror as a large piece of the cavern ceiling plummeted into the fire lake and disappeared with a glutinous splash that sent tiny red-hot particles of molten rock arcing up into the air and down around him on the path.

'Keep runnin'! Keep runnin'!' Nizkwik wailed from behind him.

'Whaddya fink I'm doin'?' Snaggi bellowed, hopping and leaping over sizzling blobs. Why did the skrawniez have to be so greedy that they'd set their cave to collapse if someone took their stupid gun without doing some sort of stupid ritual or whatever was required, when they weren't even *using* the zogging thing?

The tunnel by which they'd entered was coming up now. Another bit of ceiling rock dropped, this one only missing the path by the width of a starved snotling, and Snaggi ran on while looking upwards, hoping against hope that he wouldn't see a large bit of darkness suddenly growing in his vision, too big to avoid. Then he looked down again, panicking about tripping over something and falling headlong into the fire lake. Look up, look down, look up, look down, running all the while...

Tunnel! He clattered desperately into it, well aware that he was doomed if the ceiling started coming down in here too, but what was his alternative? He took the bends at speed, bouncing off the walls, and dived head first at the gap in the rockfall that led to the outside world. It was easier now he had a headlamp to let him see what he was doing, and he squirmed back out far more quickly than he'd made it through to begin with. He hauled himself up, ready to run on and get fully clear of the hill...

And stopped. He could see daylight now, and the threat of entombment and crushing felt considerably less. Maybe if he pulled his blasta out and waited, he could get Nizkwik as soon as he poked his ugly little head out of that hole, then get the burna and run. Yes, that was a good plan, the sort of kunnin' plan that was worthy of a grotboss. He eased his blasta free.

The barrel of the burna emerged first, pointed straight at his face. Snaggi hurriedly shoved his blasta away so that by the time Nizkwik's head emerged he was standing there innocent as you liked, without any sign of betrayal.

'Fanks for waitin'!' Nizkwik said cheerfully, extricating himself from the hole while, somehow, the barrel of the burna never quite wavered far enough away from Snaggi for him to risk going for his own weapon again. Then the other grot pulled out a piece of fur: the remnants of the skrawnie's cloak.

'Wossat for?' Snaggi asked, bewildered.

'Kunnin', eh?' Nizkwik said with a grin. He wrapped it around the burna. 'I fort da orks would be less likely to try to steal da gun from us on da way back froo da camp if dey couldn't see it!'

'Good finkin', good finkin',' Snaggi said, nodding. The blasted barrel was still a bit too close to him for comfort.

'Ya sure ya don't want me to carry it for a bit? Yoo had to get it out of dere, after all. Must be heavy.'

'Nah, it's fine,' Nizkwik said, beaming. 'Honest, I'm good. Yoo go on an' check da route back to da boss' bunker. I'll be right behind ya!'

'Right behind me. Yeah.' With few other options available, and unwilling to stay in place any longer in case this part of the hill *did* decide to collapse, Snaggi turned and led the way out while fighting the uncomfortable feeling that he'd been outwitted.

The trip back through the camp was nerve-wracking, but successful. The sun was setting, and although an ork camp was never a silent and peaceful place, a fair percentage of its inhabitants worked on the basis that going to sleep would make the next battle arrive sooner. Snaggi and Nizkwik made it through without being shot, stamped on, or harassed over the nature of the fur-wrapped bundle in Nizkwik's arms, and found Ufthak's bunker just as empty as when they'd left it some time earlier.

'Da boss must still be out huntin' skrawniez,' Nizkwik said knowledgeably. 'Dere's only a few left. We'll just have to wait for 'im.' He pointed. 'You hide in dat corner, an' I'll hide in dis one, an' den when da boss comes back...' He stroked the burna lovingly, and grinned wildly. 'Surprise time!'

Snaggi nodded, and retreated to where he had been directed. This was fine. He could still turn this to his advantage. The important thing was that Ufthak died; after that, Snaggi could slit Nizkwik's throat while the git was celebrating and claim the glory for himself!

They waited, and waited, as the sky outside darkened from blue down to black. Snaggi was just starting to think that the big boss had rumbled their scheme and was too savvy to come back into his bunker when the door opened and the massive shape of Ufthak Blackhawk strode in.

He was immense, a giant in black and yellow, one hand casually clutching the Snazzhammer, a weapon easily as tall as a humie and probably heavier. He threw it into a corner with a clatter and a grunt, and Snaggi nearly jumped at the noise. What was Nizkwik waiting for? Ufthak was going to notice them at any second, and then–

'Surprise!'

Nizkwik jumped out, gleefully brandishing the burna. Ufthak whirled around shockingly fast for something approximately the size and weight of a Killa Kan, and glowered furiously at the grot.

'Wot da zoggin' hell d'ya fink yoo're playin' at?' he thundered.

Go on! Snaggi silently urged Nizkwik. *Do it! Roast 'im, before he realises somefing's up!*

'We got ya a present, boss!' Nizkwik said happily, and he
held
the
burna
out.

Snaggi's jaw dropped, as a sucker punch of dismay, betrayal, consternation and utter fury socked him in the face. What was…? Why was…? This *wasn't fair!*

'Wot's dis?' Ufthak growled, snatching the burna from Nizkwik and peering at it. The weapon looked tiny in his massive hand.

'It's a burna, boss!' Nizkwik gushed. 'It's a skrawnie gun wot shoots *really hot* stuff dat burns gits right up!'

Ufthak grunted. Then, without apparent effort, he closed his fist and crushed the burna.

'Do I look like I want a zoggin' *skrawnie gun?*' he bellowed. 'Bloody unreliable trash, is wot dat is!' He ripped the canister off the ruined weapon and threw it at Nizkwik, hitting the grot in the chest and knocking him over. 'Dat's the fuel fingy, take it to Da Boffin an' see if he can make somefing useful wiv it. Now *get out!*' He suddenly noticed Snaggi, and his huge head whipped around to skewer him to the wall with a glare. 'An' wot are *yoo* doin' here?'

Through the sweeping despair and the tattered ruins of his ambitions, Snaggi managed to point a finger at Nizkwik. 'It was his idea!'

He lunged forward, grabbed the other grot, and towed him out of the bunker by the scruff of his neck. Ufthak slammed the door behind them, and Snaggi whirled around to press Nizkwik up against the wall.

'Wot,' he hissed, 'da *zog,* was dat?!'

Nizkwik's eyes were wide with shock. 'Wot was wot?'

The realisation hit Snaggi like a hammer. He'd been wrong. He'd been *so* wrong. He'd assumed that Nizkwik had got close to Ufthak because he was cunning, because he was scheming: because, essentially, he was like Snaggi. He couldn't have been further from the truth.

Nizkwik wasn't *pretending* to be a clueless, servile grot with the intelligence of a concussed squig; *he was exactly that.* Snaggi had grossly overestimated him, and in so doing had lost the one shot he had at taking the big boss down and seizing his destiny.

'Dis is wot I get,' he said to the galaxy in general. 'Dis is wot I get for assumin' anyone else could be even half as brilliant as me! Why am I cursed wiv greatness? *Why?*'

'Er, wot?' Nizkwik asked.

Snaggi couldn't bring himself to answer. He just turned and walked away, back out into the darkness.

Some time later, in amongst the ongoing noise and bustle that forever permeated an ork camp, the careful listener might have heard the sound of weeping, interspersed with the dull, rhythmic noise of a grot repeatedly driving his own skull into a sheet of metal out of sheer frustration.

YOUR NEXT READ

BRUTAL KUNNIN
by Mike Brooks

When Ufthak and his orks attack the forge world of Hephaesto, the last thing they want is to share the spoils with the notorious Kaptin Badrukk. But with armies to defeat and loot to seize, Ufthak's boyz might just need Badrukk's help – though that doesn't mean they can trust him...

THE WASTE, THE WORM, AND THE WITCH

GARY KLOSTER

I lay in the dark with the dead. Still, patient, silent – except for the voice in my head.

Lira thinks she has me by the throat… backstabbing coward… have her blood before the next dawn.

The words ran through my skull, vicious and angry, but I had no idea what they meant. Who was Lira? Why was she a backstabbing coward? I clenched my teeth together to keep myself from shouting those questions into the dark, and I felt the sting in my lower lip as my fangs, keen as razors, dug in. The pain didn't help.

'Quiet, Mother!' I moved my lips, but I didn't draw in any air to speak. 'Quiet, quiet, QUIET!'

No air, except for a small, hissing breath at the end so that I could breathe out those last words. They were a whisper, a scrap of sound, but they felt like a shout in the silence, and there was a rustle of bone and teeth as the dead shifted around me.

I hear something, Nyssa.

I held myself still, mouth shut so hard I could taste blood, and didn't answer. I hated it when she used my name.

From somewhere far away, beyond the dark, I heard a noise. The faint thump of footsteps, moving across the ground, the rustle of grass against someone's feet. Sounds too soft for a mortal to hear, but my senses were far keener than any human still trapped in their first life. I had got them from my father's blood, along with all the other gifts of the Soulblight.

Much better gifts than a mad voice inside my skull.

She was quiet now though, thankfully, and I focused on those footfalls, moving slowly towards where I lay. They grew louder, closer, and when the mortal stepped on the wood planks that covered me they sounded like thunder. I could see light now, thin lines of it through the boards overhead. Those lines grew and shrank as the mortal moved, prowling through the empty house above me. The trapdoors in the floor were well-hidden, but my hands tightened on the hilts of the two swords that I held. Waiting, ready. If they found those hidden doors and opened them...

My senses were one thing I inherited. My speed was another. I would be on whoever it was before they could speak.

Lira. I'm coming for you.

'Enough!'

The word hissed out of me before I could stop it. The only thing that saved me was the fact that I hadn't pulled any air in, that my lungs were empty of anything to form a shout. But still I made a sound, and the skeleton beside me clicked its teeth in response. I froze, hands tight as chains on the hilts of my blades, and listened.

The movement above me had stopped. Had they heard? I stared at the thin strips of light, so bright against the dark, and my body quivered like a bow pulled taut, ready to move. But I held myself still. This was just a scout. Not all the mortals were in the trap yet, and I wanted all the Sun Seekers, not just a portion of them.

I held myself still, even as my mother began to shout in my head.

Do you hear me! I'm coming for you, and I'm not going to stop until your blood stains my teeth!

Not far over my head, the footsteps began to move away. Not creeping, not running, but moving at a normal walk, and I held myself still. Maybe Mother hadn't ruined this for us. The scout moved, stepping onto the grassy village green that lay outside the house I was hiding beneath. Then there was a voice.

'It's empty!'

She sounded young and excited, as if she had run off the farmers who had called this place their home all by herself. She wouldn't be excited for long.

There were a few moments of silence, outside and in my head, and then the sound of many more boots, mixed with the sounds of hooves. Not many, though. The Sun Seekers had lost most of their cavalry ten years ago at Ire Crossing, when they'd first shown their hand on the Broken Plains and attacked us. The fact that they had hit us by surprise was the only reason they hadn't lost all their cavalry and more.

Today I meant to repay that ambush.

Backstabbing coward.

'Empty?' Another woman's voice, but she sounded wary, not excited.

'They ran from us,' said the scout. 'Or the bloodsuckers took them. Probably the–'

There was a thin, twanging sound, and the scout's voice cut off with a grunt. There were shouts, the sound of feet running, the wary woman barking orders. Then the sound of steel cracking against bone. They'd found the skeletal archer I'd left for them, hidden in the thatched roof of one of the houses.

'Burn it,' the woman barked.

'You heard Lieutenant Takora,' a man shouted. 'Burn them all!'

Takora. I smiled to myself. I'd fought her twice before, and she'd slipped away both times. I shifted my blades, getting ready. She wouldn't get away today.

Have her throat.

'Quiet,' I breathed, letting the words out now. There were running feet and shouts and the crackle of flames starting outside, and I could at least give vent to a whisper now. Soon. Soon. In my chest, my heart gave a single beat, stirring the cold blood in my veins as my body prepared itself. I reached out with the magic in my blood and touched the dead around me. Pale grave light flared up from dim points in empty eye sockets. Then, drifting down from the cracks above, the first tendrils of smoke came. They'd set the house above alight.

Fire…

'Don't,' I said as the air around me stirred, beginning to grow hot, and light began to pour through the floorboards.

Fire, Nyssa. Run!

With a snarl I moved, springing up at the hidden door over me. It flew open and I was in the empty house above, the flames just beginning to roll across the ceiling. Smoke wrapped around me, and sparks touched my skin like tiny knives, but I was out, racing into the open, where the Sun Seekers stood in their orange uniforms, staring at the burning buildings. The ones closest to me flinched back as I burst out of the door, a dark shadow bearing two swords, one flashing in the firelight, one dark as the smoke boiling up overhead. They stared at me, shocked, and that second of surprise was all the time I needed. My heart was beating steady now, every thump moving and heating my blood, and I was fast as the wind.

Two fell, my bright blade carving through one's throat while my dark blade drove up under the other's ribs and into their heart. Neither made a sound as they fell, but when I spun and slammed the hilt of one of my swords into the temple of another they shrieked, the painful scream filling the night.

The scream was good. I wanted the Sun Seekers' attention focused on me, and on the line of skeletons pouring out of the burning house behind me. I could see their angular shadows dancing across the soldiers' faces as I kept moving, blocking a sword and kicking off a shield that swung at me, throwing myself back from the soldiers rushing me and letting them smash into the skeletons. I paused for a second, watching as Sun Seekers and skeletal warriors tangled together, weapons striking. There were maybe three dozen mortal soldiers, and they were going to overwhelm the twenty skeletons my father had made and sent with me – the dead warriors were implacable, but even those made by a king were not exactly skilled. But behind the Sun Seekers I could see more skeletons rushing out of the other burning houses, behind two dark figures. Rill and Erant, the guards given to me by my father, the king, whether

I wanted them or not. Rill was already launching arrow after arrow into the backs of the Sun Seekers, while Erant charged forward, his greatsword cutting through soldiers like a scythe. The mortals were caught now, and Lieutenant Takora was shouting from the top of her horse, trying to get them to withdraw, to fight their way out and away. I started to run, moving to cut them off.

Run! Run! The fire… I'm burning!

'You burned, Vasara, now keep quiet about it,' I hissed as I streaked past the skeletons. But she didn't, of course.

Burning! I'm burning!

Her voice echoed through my head, on the edge of a scream. Damn it, she hadn't screamed when she had died. She'd been too busy murdering that treacherous mortal who had tricked us into an ambush that… Well, that was almost exactly the same as the ambush I had set for the Sun Seekers.

'Vasara's dead,' I snapped, 'and you're just some idiot noise in my head and you have to quiet yourself!' I was almost around the skeletons, heading towards the knot of mortals desperately fighting their way out of the trap, but the voice in my head wasn't listening, she was only getting louder.

Burning, burning, burning!

My mother's voice filled my head, drowning out everything, and with it came a flood of light and a rush of heat and pain. I staggered to a halt, convinced I'd somehow run into one of the burning houses. But it was just Mother, her voice filling me, somehow dragging me into the memory of her death – or a hallucination of it. I stood where I was, imaginary fire roaring around me. I knew it wasn't real, but the pain was still there, searing through me.

'Get out!' I shouted. 'It was my fault, I know, but get out of my head!' The flames didn't subside, though, not for what felt like forever, not until my mother's voice finally went silent in my head.

I stood in the centre of the burned-out ruin of the village, surrounded by smouldering coals and smoking thatch. The surviving skeletons stood in neat ranks, and the corpses of the Sun Seekers, raised by Rill and Erant, stood silent beside them. It looked like we had got almost all of them, except for the few mounted troops. Including their lieutenant, who had escaped me again. I stared at them all, then silently cleaned my swords and sheathed them.

'Are you all right, Lady Nyssa?' Erant asked cautiously.

Nothing's all right.

The words whispered through my head like a chill breeze, and I had to clench my teeth again to keep from screaming.

'Enough,' I said, to her, to him, to everything, and I turned and started to walk away.

The Grey Palace sat nestled at the foot of Mount Temero, the massive volcano that towered over the dry grasslands of the Broken Plains. The Grey Palace was where the Crimson Keep, the cursed home of the Kastelai, had appeared almost a century ago, bringing Mother, Father, me, and all the other vampires bound to that place. Then the Keep had vanished again, disappearing almost as quickly as it had come, taking almost all of those it had brought with it.

But not us. Not the ones that had ridden out too far, the ones who couldn't make it back before the Crimson Keep had gone so suddenly. My strange little adopted family and a handful of others were abandoned here, in this forgotten corner of Aqshy. But we'd not only survived, we'd thrived. We'd taken control of the ruins of the Grey Palace and the mortal city of Maar, crowned the man I called Father, Corsovo

Volari, king, and declared the Broken Plains ours. And they almost were. Until the Sun Seekers had come.

'We should ask her.'

I stood at the windows in the reception room of my apartment in the Grey Palace, staring at the boiling lake that stretched out towards the distant Maar. My back was to Rill and Erant, but it was easy to hear them talk even if they were keeping their voices in low whispers.

'Do what you want, Erant,' Rill said. 'But she doesn't want to hear it.'

I didn't. I didn't want to hear their questions about what was happening in my head any more than I wanted to hear that voice that I'd been cursed with.

He didn't speak to me. He never does, any more. What is wrong?

'You're dead,' I said. My lips moved, but I didn't draw in any air to speak the words. 'That's why he doesn't talk to you. So why in all the hells do you keep talking to me?'

Father. My hand tightened into a fist, and I ground my knuckles into the stone edge of the window. He'd congratulated me over the success of the ambush, but I could barely speak to him. How many years would it take before I could face him without the feeling of failure churning through me? He didn't blame me for Vasara's death, but he should have. I was her bodyguard when we'd gone to meet that treacherous mortal who had killed her. I should have pulled her from those flames before she burned. I should have killed the man before he'd sprung the trap. I should have–

'Lady Nyssa. Are you all right?' Erant had moved closer before he spoke to me, but not too close. He had come to know me well enough to have some caution. Still, my speed surprised him at times, and he blinked when I went from standing with my back to him, staring out the window, to standing right before him, staring into his face from inches away.

'All right?' I said, my words quiet but hard. 'Don't I look all right?'

I was tall, but Erant was taller, and his shoulders were broader, his muscles heavier. But he kept himself very carefully still. He might be larger than me, stronger, but the gift of blood that my father had given me was strong in my veins. My senses were keener than his; I could wrap myself in silence like a cloak; I could heal quickly, even compared to other vampires; and I was fast. So fast that whenever I sparred with Erant, I could leave a dozen blade-marks on his skin before I even had to bother with ducking his first blow.

'You look…' He trailed off, uncertain of what to say, and threw a pleading glance over his shoulder at Rill.

'He's worried about what happened at the village,' Rill said.

I stared at my bodyguard, looking at the reflection of my eyes in his. They were brown, just a little darker than my skin but lighter than the black of my hair, and marked with red lines that grew larger after I had fed. Or when I was angry. Right now, my irises were more red than brown, and I could see that Erant was regretting saying anything. As he should.

'Don't worry about that,' I said. 'Worry about annoying me.'

'I don't want to,' Erant said. 'But your father said we were to help you however we could, and–'

'You can't help me with this,' I said, cutting him off. 'Unless you know a necromancer.' Would an exorcism work? Was she a ghost? Or just my own madness? I didn't know, and I couldn't. Father had been looking for a necromancer for years, but the few mages living on the Broken Plains barely had the talent to light a grass fire in the dry season. None of them had any talent with the amethyst magic of death.

Why won't he speak to me?

'Why won't you be quiet?' I told her as I turned from Erant, but I said it out loud. I had no problem with him thinking that it was meant for him.

'I know one.'

Rill's voice came across the room and made me stop. I looked over at her, and she shrugged.

'At least some of the stories say she can speak to the dead,' she said.

'Who?' I asked.

'The Witch of the Waste.'

It was easy to get away from the palace. Just tell the mortal servants to saddle up Thorn, my Nightmare mount, and leave. It was impossible to get away from Erant and Rill, though. But at least this time they would serve a purpose.

Well. Rill would.

'Where is she?'

I'd stopped us on one of Temero's high ridges. We'd taken the narrow trail up this flank of the volcano and after long hours of climbing, the land spread out like a map below us. On one side the Grey Palace lay far below, set between the volcano and the boiling stretch of Irewater Lake. At its other end stood Maar, and spreading out beyond the city were rolling brown hills that led down to flatlands that stretched to the distant sea. The Broken Plains, in all their dull, dusty glory.

The land on the other side of the volcano was so much worse, though.

It was a flat plain, marred with lava flows both ancient and new, some still smoking beneath their craggy black surfaces. Between the flows stretched vast shallow lakes, the waters shining with metallic poisons, and grey mudflats that bubbled and stank. Below us, I could see where our trail split. One fork led to the fortress of Ruinwatch, which guarded this barren wasteland. The other ran down the volcano and disappeared into the wastes.

Where I was going, hunting a story to answer a hallucination.

'Are you sure she's out there?' I asked. Again.

'My grandfather said he met her,' Rill said. 'I believed him.'

'Was she a beautiful maiden? Or a hideous crone?' Erant asked. 'I've heard both.'

'He said she looked like his sister,' Rill said. 'Just muddier. She gave him goat stew and cured the tumours that were eating him alive. But she drowned the other two that came with him in boiling mud.'

'Why?' Erant asked.

'She didn't say and he didn't ask,' Rill said. 'The stories all say she helps only a few and kills the rest.'

So much grey. I should have worn my black gown.

I ignored the voice and tapped Thorn, sending the Nightmare down the trail, heading towards the fork that led to the wastes. Help or kill. That would probably be how it went. My hand went to the hilt of my bright sword. But I wouldn't be the one to die.

It took days to find her, and in the end it was my hunger that led me to her.

I caught the scent of her blood one morning as we picked our way across another rough lava flow, leading the Nightmares around lava tubes that carved through the stones like empty veins. I smelled it and I turned to follow. It was either

her or some fool mortal on the same quest we were, and if it was the latter we'd feed and move on.

I was so hungry I was almost disappointed that it turned out to be her.

She was a woman of middle age, dressed in shabby clothes, her face seamed with ash, her boots grubby with mud. The witch looked plain, ordinary, except for the polished chunks of obsidian woven into her hair and the strange grey bones strung around her neck. She carried nothing with her: no weapons, not even a stick, and no possessions. There was no sign of a house or shelter nearby. She seemed to just be there, surviving on nothing but poison air and toxic mud.

'Finally,' she said when we walked towards her, each of us leashing the beast in our blood that snarled with hunger at the sight of her.

'Finally?' I reined in Thorn, staring at her. My eyes were fixed on her neck, on the veins running beneath her skin. It felt hard to speak, with every bit of my will holding me still, keeping me from killing her. 'If you were waiting, you could have come to us instead of letting us wander for days.'

'But the waiting is part of it,' she said. She raised a hand, and in her palm I saw a pile of tiny, dried bones, carved with symbols. The vertebrae of snakes and birds and lizards, the crude fortune-telling tools the nomads living beyond the Broken Plains used. 'It gives me time to see what you want, and it gives me time to judge the cost of it.'

The cost is life. The cost is vengeance. The cost is blood.

I shook my head, as if the voice were a fly buzzing around my ears. 'You know what I want?' I asked. 'Tell me.' I looked at the pile of bones in her hand, worn and dirty. 'Prove to me you're not just a brush mage, working charms for nomads.'

'You want me to prove myself to you, Nyssa Volari?' she asked. 'You want me to prove myself, to show that I have the ability to pull the voice of the woman you call Mother out of your head?'

'You see her? Hear her?' I said, my hunger for blood shoved away by a different need. 'Is she really there?'

'I see your problem,' the witch said. 'I hear your need. But I'll give you nothing, until my price is paid.'

'Your price.' Rill said her grandfather had paid for his healing with a good new knife. The witch's price in stories ranged, from something as common as a spoon to a whisker from Sigmar's beard. I'd brought trade pearls and realmstone, a small fortune in each. And some spoons. 'What do you want?'

'A fang,' she said, and then smiled, showing me her yellow teeth. 'Not yours. I want a mudworm fang, one longer than your longest finger.'

'What's a mudworm?' I asked, and she pointed to a distant rocky crag of black stone.

'At the base of that stone there is a lake. Go there, and you will find them.' Her smile became a laugh. 'Truthfully, they will find you!'

The cost is blood.

That voice in my head, and my hunger, and the witch and her way of speaking to me as if I were an especially stupid child. It was all I could do to keep myself from tearing her throat out. But I kept my beast leashed, for now.

'I bring you the tooth, and you'll rid me of this damned voice?'

'Pay my price, and I will help you,' she replied, an answer without an answer, and I wanted to kill her. But–

The cost is blood.

'Quiet,' I snapped, then started Thorn towards the distant black stone, away from the witch and her laughter.

The lake was there at the base of the black stone tower, vast but shallow. Its water was achingly blue, stretched across mud that was white as clouds. It was as beautiful as the sky and filled the air around it with the scent of bitter poison.

'This seems like a bad idea,' Erant said, staring out at the smooth water.

'It is a bad idea,' I told him. The day was bright, and the toxic water gleamed with light, making my eyes ache. I slid off Thorn and drew my swords. 'So is telling me that it's a bad idea.'

I walked to the edge of the lake. The water was still except for a few tiny ripples from the warm breeze. The mud gave a little beneath my feet, but it was firm underneath, and I left only shallow tracks. Maybe it wouldn't ruin my boots, I thought, as I stepped into the poison water. I heard Rill and Erant following, the splash of their feet in the lake, but I ignored it. Water rose to my ankles, then up my shins, warm as a bath, but nothing happened.

I was a few hundred paces from the shore, the water barely to my knees, before the first mudworm appeared. It was simple and hideous, a length of white mud rising from the water like a blunt tentacle. It had no features, no eyes or nose or anything, just a white tube that swayed in the air before me. I spun my swords and watched it, and then another surfaced. And another, and another, and another, popping up out of the water all around us. They swayed, their ends angled towards us, the only indication that we had that they knew we were there. I watched them, silent, frowning. There was no blood smell to them, which meant a fight with no feeding.

How then will you keep the beast at bay?

'With violence,' I snarled and stepped forward, stabbing out with my bright sword.

The gleaming blade hit the mudworm and slid in, almost as easily as stabbing water. Its edge cut through the snake-like body and came out the other side. A few sluggish ripples rolled away from where my blade transfixed it, and when those ripples reached the blunt end of the mudworm they rebounded. They grew and became fissures in the white mud. Those fissures split, peeling back like torn skin. The end of the mudworm opened like a wound, revealing row after row of shining teeth like blue glass. Those teeth clinked and chimed as the thing twisted on my sword, lunging forward, lashing at me like a living flail with splinters of sharp, shining fangs.

I twisted my hand holding the bright sword and threw off the thing's strike. Swinging my dark sword around, I sliced through the mudworm, cutting it in half. It fell into the water with a splash, the writhing tendrils of its end lashing, trying to catch me with its cutting teeth. I skipped back, watching as the base of the worm fell into the water. Then I was spinning, facing the next as it came lunging in.

Cut and slash, move and dodge. I danced through the tentacles, the poisonous water splashing around me as I cut the mudworms apart. They were numerous, but slow and soft, and it was easy, so easy.

Too easy.

I cut through another one and swung away. My heart thrummed a slow, steady beat, and I was moving fast, fast enough to dodge another strike and pull clear of the fight, getting space enough to see what was going on. Erant was marked with a few cuts on his face, but he was hewing through the worms surrounding him with vast swings of his blade. Rill had slung her bow away and had her knife out, a blade almost as long as a short sword, viciously hooked. She was cutting through the mudworms with it, but her face was grim.

'They don't die!' she shouted, and she was right. Out of the fight, I could see it now. Erant cut the deadly, toothy ends off three of the things in one swing, and they splashed down into the water. Only to fumble around until they found a severed end to fuse to, and then they rose up again.

I cursed as the mudworm I had sliced in half a few seconds ago rose again from the water, ripped its end open and came at me, glass teeth shining. I cut it down and moved, but two more replaced it, and as I dealt with them I could see the first pulling itself back together. These things, whatever they were, were as deathless as we were. This fight was futile.

I slammed my bright sword back into its sheath, freeing a hand. When the next mudworm attacked, I slashed through its soft white body with my black blade and then caught the thrashing head with my free hand. Glass teeth bit into my palm, but I ignored the pain as I held the awful thing away from me, keeping the other lashing bits of its jaws back. I started towards the shore with my prize, cutting down the other mudworms that tried to stop me. The glass fangs digging into my palm weren't even close to the length the witch had demanded, but they were going to have to do. None of these things had fangs that long, and I wasn't going to be cut to ribbons by the unkillable monstrosities looking for one that did.

But it came looking for me.

Suddenly, the snapping pack of mudworms went still as sticks, frozen in place around us. Then they all fell back into the water, disappearing into the white mud. The thrashing piece I held dissolved in my hand, mud running through my fingers like blood, carrying with it the jagged glass teeth. I grabbed at them, plucking one small blue triangle from the air, but it cracked and broke in my grip, leaving me snarling at a useless handful of glittering dust.

The beast, the beast…

'What beast, Mother?' I shouted. My voice rang out over the empty water. Rill and Erant stared at me, confused, but I didn't care. 'The beast in my blood? It's starving. The witch's monsters? They've all run off. It's just me in the mud, listening to you gibber, and maybe that's it? Maybe you're the beast, haunting my head forever, my punishment for getting you killed. Is that it?'

The poisoned land soaked up my words and gave me back silence. Silence finally broken by one word whispered through my head, an almost silent question.

Killed?

Then the water exploded up beside me.

A twisting body, thick as my torso, reared up over the lake, a mudworm five times the size of the others. Its blunt, blind head turned down to face me, and then the tip of the thing tore itself open into a dozen writhing strips of lashing white, each one studded with shards of blue glass the length of my hand.

Here were the fangs I needed, ten thousand of them, flashing in the light as the thing lunged towards me. I dived to the side, avoiding the strike. The thing was slow, awkward, but huge. Its jaws, tongues, tendrils, whatever they were, lashed after me and I felt a fang slash through my armour, slicing into my back, bumping over shoulder blade and vertebra. I felt the hot rush of blood against my skin, the painful touch of air on exposed tissue, then my flesh knitted itself closed. But that healing, combined with the pounding thrum of my heart, was burning through the strength left in me. I was starved for blood, for life, and I needed it now as the giant mudworm reared again, ready to smash itself down at me once more.

Then Rill and Erant hit it. Rill had her bow out; her hands were a blur as she fitted arrow after arrow to the string, pulled it back and sent them slamming into the twisting white body. Erant was swinging his greatsword into the beast like a woodsman attacking a tree, the huge blade gouging massive slashes in the mudworm's hide.

Their attack made the worm twist its glass-toothed head around to stare down at them. Rill took the chance and fired half a dozen arrows into the beast's fanged maw, but it took no more notice of those arrows than it had of the ones she'd shot into its body. The mudworm swung back around, turning away from them, spread the ragged fringe of its tendrils wide, then struck.

I tried to do my trick again, to sever one of the toothed tentacles that the mudworm swung at me, but when my blade struck, it only dug halfway through. The cut tendril was thrown off a little, wrapping around my sword-arm instead of my neck, but it still caught me tight, glass fangs biting deep, and my blood marked its white hide.

Kill. Killing. Killed. Killed.

The words ran through my head, a whisper of sound I couldn't stop. I hissed in pain and frustration, trying to draw my bright blade with my free hand as the mudworm tightened its grip on my arm, glass teeth stabbing through skin and muscle to grind on the bones of my forearm. I kicked out with a leg, driving it into the thing's soft body, trying to free myself from its grasp, heedless of the teeth tearing through my flesh, but it was too strong.

Killed. Death. Death. Killing, oh killing death, death killing.

'Quiet,' I grated through my teeth as I jerked my bright blade out of its scabbard. I was being shredded by this thing, and all I could hear was her ranting and it was driving me mad. With my sword free I cut at the mudworm, but I couldn't sever the thick tentacle that held me. It was drawing me in, no matter that I was shoving back with both feet now, and it was going to tear me apart.

Kill me.

Killed me.

Then Erant was there, charging forward, his greatsword flying down. The huge blade slammed through the twisting limb and cut it. Suddenly free, I flew back, landing in the brilliant blue water. I twisted the moment I hit, getting my boots under me, driving myself up out of the water. I saw Erant backing up, cutting through tentacles as they swung towards him, saw Rill behind him shooting at the thing, driving arrow after arrow into the base of the tentacles, slowing and tangling them. Turned and saw the black rock soaring up behind us.

'Move!' I shouted to them and headed for it.

The water dropped as we ran, from knees to shins to ankles, and we were on the dry white dirt. Behind us the mudworm reared up as if it could see us with its blunt, eyeless head. Then it slipped back down into the mud beneath the shallow water and disappeared, leaving me with an arm covered in blood and white mud, studded with long, broken fangs of blue glass.

Killed, my mother whispered in my pain-hazed thoughts as I pulled out the largest fang and held it in front of me. *Dead.*

'Not today,' I said. 'Not me. Just you.'

Just you.

There was a tangle of emotions wrapped in those words that I couldn't sort out, then she was gone, and for once she was finally quiet.

'Here, witch.' I held up the fang, a length of jagged blue glass longer than my hand, its tip stained with my blood. 'I've done my part. Now do yours.'

The woman was sitting on a flat rock beside a great pool of grey mud bubbling slowly beneath the light of the dying day. She hadn't looked up as we approached, focused instead on carefully arranging her collection of carved bones in an intricate pattern around her. But when I spoke her eyes came up and fastened to the gleaming fang.

'Ah,' she said softly and held out her hand. 'I knew. Even though something in their magic keeps their fates hidden from me, I knew you could defeat the mudworms.'

I bit back a bitter laugh before it could spill out of my mouth. Let the witch think we'd won.

'I brought your price. Now prove to me it was worth the effort, or I'm going to use this to cut your throat.'

The witch smiled. 'Nyssa Volari. Cursed to hear your mother Vasara's voice echoing in your head, for as long as your unnatural life lasts. But does that mean you're possessed by her ghost? Or is it the memory of her, made by your own mind? The answer is simple. It doesn't matter. What matters is that she is there, and you must make your peace with her and her death. And she must do the same.'

I stared at her, gripping the fang so hard it cut into my palm. 'Is that all?'

She nodded, and I stepped forward, my boots almost brushing her carefully arranged bones.

'I asked for magic, for relief, for silence in my head. And you give me nothing but useless, useless words!' I put the fang against her throat and the edge of it drew a thin line of blood.

'All I can give you I already have given,' she said. 'If that's not enough–'

'It's not,' I said, and pressed the fang in.

She moved as I did. Not away from the cutting edge, but closer, driving her throat into my thrust. Her skin parted, and the vessels beneath ruptured, spilling hot blood across my hand. My hunger surged in me, and my hands flashed out, catching her by the front of her dusty dress. I pulled her close, mouth opening, but as I drew her in I felt her weight shifting, moving away from me. The witch was dissolving, her body transforming into white mud that ran out of her clothes and splashed onto the rock below. The carved bones were caught in it, washed over the stone's edge into the pool of boiling mud. White mud and bones mixed with the bubbling grey, and for a moment the white seemed to draw a symbol across the surface, all jagged points and curves. And then it sank, dissolving away, lost in the grey.

I was left clutching a handful of dirty clothes and a necklace of bones. I threw them down and licked at the bit of blood that still clung to my skin. The taste of it made my hunger grow, and I had to hold myself still, staring across the wastes at nothing.

'That was–' Rill started, but I held up my hand, silencing her. My anger was so close, ready to explode, but in that quiet a voice came.

I'm dead, aren't I?

'You are,' I said.

But not gone, it seems.

'It seems not.' Her voice was quiet in my head, and different. It was... aware. Not raving. 'Can you? Be gone?'

No. There was a long pause. *This is not ideal.*

'What, you screaming gibberish in my head? No, it's not.'

I've come back to myself. That's done. But I'm still here. I don't know how, or why, but I am, and I may always be.

But sane now. And coherent. That was something, wasn't it? I'd have her in my head, forever. Watching me, making comments on what I was doing, giving advice. Just as she had in life, but there would be no escape now, ever. I closed my eyes, tipped back my head, and screamed. The sound echoed off the broken rocks, and I stood still, waiting for silence.

Feel better?

'Quiet,' I said, as cold and calm as I could, barely holding back another scream. Then I kicked the witch's clothes into the mud, walked back to Thorn, mounted up, and started for home with Rill and Erant following. Moving in a silence that I knew, now, was never, ever going to last.

YOUR NEXT READ

THE LAST VOLARI
by Gary Kloster

A doomed vampire faces down the nature of her curse, and the righteous fury of the faithful of Sigmar.

THE SHEL'TAIN AFFAIR

JUDE REID

Humanity is a superstitious species. Old notions of faith and fate are carried in our flesh like parasites, weighing us down as we strive to transcend the shackles of the past. Our minds have evolved to seek meaning in the patterns of random chance, and if history is to be believed, we find those patterns with tiresome regularity. Perhaps the search for greater meaning lies at the heart of what makes us human, and it is only once we overcome that part of our nature that we will achieve our true potential.

And yet, as the blast of the exploding groundcar took me from my feet and threw me across the windswept clifftop like a doll hurled by an angry child, all I could think of was the sheer arbitrariness of my own survival. A superstitious woman would have seen the hand of fate in that moment, even come to believe that she had survived through some caprice of destiny or the will of an imagined god. But I knew better. The fact I was still alive was the result of my own actions and of random chance, nothing more or less than that.

I was in no doubt as to what had just happened – the brand that Malcador the Sigillite had placed so recently on the skin of my palm might as well have been a target painted between my shoulder blades – but even so, questions flooded my mind like rushing water. *Who* had ordered my death was not in question. Here in the isolated and windswept Shel'tain territories, no one but the High Duke possessed the audacity, or the means.

The more interesting question was *why*.

I had arrived on Shel'tain less than six hours before, and had been met at the landing site by the High Duke himself in an elegant steel-grey groundcar. As the newly made Agentia Tertius of Lord Malcador, I supposed I should have expected nothing less, but my title was fresh enough that the deference and respect it brought with it were strange after a life of interactions characterised by fear and revulsion. The instinctive repugnance that everyone felt in my presence persisted, of course, but it was curious to see it masked by a veneer of courtesy.

'Welcome to Shel'tain, Lady Amendera.' The High Duke's voice was low, but contained a sharp edge that cut across the rising wind. 'We are honoured by your visit. What service can our humble house offer you?'

I let the breeze take his words and regarded him in silence. High Duke Ceithyr of Shel'tain was a lean, well-preserved man in his late middle age, with upswept silver hair and eyes the precise colour of the dull grey rock beneath his feet. He wore a suit of mesh armour as fine as my own, with a brindled fur mantle draped nonchalantly around his shoulders. His mouth curved in a smile of welcome that betrayed no trace of the revulsion he must have felt in my proximity. This was a man whose family had weathered the storms of Terra for a thousand years, and he looked every inch the part.

'Lord Malcador has sent me to inspect your holdings.' I took a step towards him, wondering if he would recoil, but he stood his ground. 'He wishes to ascertain the nature and extent of your loyalty to the Emperor.'

'Of course.' The High Duke inclined his head. 'I am at your disposal.'

Silence fell again. Since leaving the Silent Sisterhood – an order of witch-seekers, charged with eradicating all sorcerous threats to the Imperium – I found the endless chatter that surrounded me tiresome and draining. I had quickly learned that most individuals were unable to resist filling the gaps in conversation, and consequently could be relied upon to spill all manner of inappropriate confidences. Much to my inconvenience, however, it seemed the High Duke was possessed of steel within as well as without.

It took a full three hours to inspect the Shel'tain holdings, and by the end of the tour I was left with the impression that I had barely scratched the surface. The complex was squat and ugly, somewhere between a factorum and a fortress, clinging to the edge of a grey granite cliff. Centuries ago, Shel'tain had been an island chain whose settlements overlooked a vast ocean, but now the plain below the promontory stretched to the far horizon in an infinite expanse of white sand. Thin northern sunlight glinted across a silver net of cables connected to an array of geothermal lances driven deep into Terra's crust. The planet's resources might be all but spent, but the fires burning at its heart were still a font of limitless power for those with the means to harvest them.

'May I offer you refreshments, Lady Amendera?' the High Duke asked, when we had returned to the great stone portico where we had begun the tour hours before.

I waved his offer away and tried to conceal my frustration. What was the man hiding? In my brief tenure as Lord Malcador's bloodhound, I had found few individuals who displayed the High Duke's remarkable degree of composure. The mere mention of the Sigillite should have sent even the innocent into paroxysms of self-doubt, but the High Duke displayed only effortless confidence.

'Then allow me to extend the invitation to explore my home as you see fit. I would have you return to Lord Malcador secure in the knowledge that Shel'tain's loyalty is beyond reproach.'

My thoughts scrabbled for purchase on what was rapidly turning into an insoluble problem. The High Duke might well have omitted areas of his holdings from the tour he had so generously provided, but I had seen no signs of hidden doors or false walls that hinted at secret passageways. Short of pulling on every sconce and bookcase in the building, I had no idea where I would even start to look. Leaving now and returning later with soldiers was another option, but I feared that Lord Malcador would take a dim view of destruction wreaked on an ally whose crimes were yet unproven.

But that was the problem: there *was* no proof. Shel'tain had declared its loyalty to the Emperor early in His wars of Unification, and as His star had risen, so too had the Shel'tain family's. Rivals had fallen away, one after another, perishing with startling regularity each time they might have stood in the High Duke's way, though never with any evidence to link the family to the deaths. In more superstitious times, such relentless prosperity in the face of overwhelming hardship might have been considered a mark of divine favour, but I had been sent here in search of a more rational explanation. It was clear that Malcador suspected Shel'tain of *something*, but he had declined to share his reasons when he dispatched me to find out more.

Not for the first time, I found myself wondering why my lord had sent me rather than any one of a dozen more suitable agents. My presence here sent a clear message to the High Duke – that if evidence of his guilt was found, the wrath of the Sigillite would be swift and merciless – but I could not shake the feeling that there was something more to it than that. My mentor had been clear that I was here to investigate, not to punish, and that I would need more than my battlefield skills if I were to succeed.

I rather feared that the High Duke was not the only one being tested.

The door swung open, and a young woman in grey household livery walked briskly to the High Duke's side. As she whispered into his ear, Lord Ceithyr's expression changed to one of doubt, irritation and – there it was – an unmistakable hint of fear. His serene mask of confidence reasserted itself immediately, but the damage was already done. The High Duke was hiding something, just as Malcador had suspected.

All I had to do was find out what.

That turned out to be easier in principle than in practice. I spent another two fruitless hours prowling the citadel, the huge steel doors that separated one section from the next parting obediently at my approach. The household staff were dutiful and courteous, permitting me access to the gardens, the servants' quarters, even the vast turbine chamber beneath the great hall, all of which showed no sign of wrongdoing. I could not shake the image of skating over ice floes, the dark and hungry water waiting beneath my feet.

When I had walked through the tapestried hall for the third time, I knew I was defeated. I was, as I had known from the outset, the wrong agent for this task, and all that was left for me to do was to return in failure.

The High Duke was the soul of civility as he bade me farewell, offering me the use of his groundcar and its driver to return to my Arvus lighter. I accepted without thinking, my mind a tangle of second-guessed suspicions, fears and worries as we sped along the clifftop road. From the back of the vehicle, I watched the tech-fortress receding through armaglass fogged with condensation and stippled with rain-drops, as if my gaze alone could force it to give up its secrets. Then, as the groundcar rattled over a pothole, the sudden jolt broke my chain of thought. I looked up to see the driver leaning forward, one hand reaching under his chair. His eyes were fixed on the road, but the tension in his shoulders was unmistakable. He was ready to move.

I reacted a second too late. Before I could grab the pistol on my belt, the groundcar screeched to a halt, the deceleration sending me slamming against the back of the seat in front. A slug punched a hole in the cushion where my head had been a moment ago, filling the air with smoke, stuffing and the scent of cordite. I drew my autopistol and took a blind shot through the driver's seat, then threw my weight against the side door. It burst open, and I rolled to the ground, scrambled back to my feet and tore open the driver's door. The man was still in his seat, the front of his uniform stained scarlet with blood, his face an ugly shade of grey. I grabbed his collar and dragged him out of the vehicle, slammed his back against the external plating and lifted him so his eyes were level with mine. They widened with panic, the discomfort of my proximity enough to cut through even the horror of his approaching death.

'The High Duke.' I loosened my grip a fraction so that he could draw a laboured breath through bloody lips. 'What is he hiding?'

The driver shook his head. I clamped my hand around his windpipe so suddenly that his eyes visibly bulged.

'Tell me or die.'

The threat rang hollow. What sense was there in intimidating an already dying man? I could tell from his smile that he knew that as well as I did. He opened his hand and let a small metallic object drop to the ground.

A detonator.

His lips moved, but the time for talking was past. Still gripping him by the neck I turned and ran, his body held behind me like a shield–

And the groundcar exploded.

I woke to a burning world.

With no clearer sense of direction than 'away', I crawled on hands and knees until the fiery heat in my lungs eased, then looked back at the wreckage of the groundcar. From the state of its remains – a blazing tangle of twisted metal and shattered armaglass – the explosive charge had been a sizeable one, most likely positioned below the engine block. My suit of golden chain armour had done much to absorb and deflect the energy of the blast, and the driver's body had provided an additional layer of protection. Only his scattered remains were recognisable: an arm, still covered in the sleeve of a steel-grey tunic; a splintered rack of ribs; a severed head lying face down in the dirt.

I took another painful breath and tried to steady my racing heart. My lungs ached as though I had been exposed to vacuum, my ears still ringing with the blast, my mouth full of the taste of copper and ash. I ran my hands over my scalp and brought them away covered in the charred remains of my close-cropped black hair. There was a fresh laceration over my right eye – a new battle scar for the aquila on my forehead – and a latticework of shallow cuts stood out in vivid crimson against the skin of my hands.

I made a quick evaluation of my assets and found them woefully limited. My pistol and dagger had survived the explosion unscathed, but my vox-bead had slipped free of my ear at some point during my involuntary flight and was now one unidentifiable shard of metal amongst a hundred. I thought of my sword, safely stored on the Arvus, and a pang of regret shot through me. I had feared that arriving on a diplomatic mission with an executioner greatblade slung across my back might leave the High Duke with altogether the wrong impression of my intentions, but now its absence felt like a missing limb.

What would a trained agent do?

My options were narrowing by the moment. I could strike out for my lander on foot, but that was an unappealing prospect that gave the advantage to those with local knowledge and access to transport. The clifftop was a stark expanse of granite that promised neither shelter nor concealment, and all the combat training of my years in the Silent Sisterhood would not protect me when the High Duke's soldiers came in force. Survival seemed impossible.

But then, I had survived impossible odds before.

I thought back to my days on Luna and the hours spent beneath the shimmering domes of the Somnus Citadel. I might be all but unarmed, but I could be every bit as quick and devious as the High Duke himself, no matter how far superior his weapons or extensive his reach. And when fighting an enemy whose reach exceeds your own, the only way to win is to close the distance and get inside their guard.

I shot a glance to the cliff edge and my stomach gave a lurch. My only route of escape lay down the rocky escarpment, and from the roar of an approaching engine, it seemed there was no time to waste. Keeping low to the ground, I half ran, half crawled through the smoky air towards the ledge. For a second, I had the irrational instinct that I had arrived at the edge of the world, with only a long drop into nothingness ahead of me. The fine white sand gleamed far below, promising a swift death for any fool clumsy enough to fall.

Lumen-beams cut through the mist: dirtcycles, two of them. I dropped flat on my belly, swung myself over the ledge and instantly regretted it as the world fell away beneath me. I fixed my gaze on the cliff face and fought back panic, forcing myself to move one hand, one foot and one breath at a time.

Above me, voices drifted back and forth in the wind, fading in and out of audibility.

'How long are we supposed to wait?' a woman said. From her tone she was making little effort to hide her frustration.

Her companion sounded calmer, and considerably closer. 'Until the fire burns low enough to check for another body inside.'

I risked a look up and saw a pair of booted feet, a cloud of falling lho-ash stirred to eddies by the wind. If whoever was standing there looked down, they could hardly fail to see me. Taking care not to dislodge the rocks, I lifted my right hand and pulled my pistol from its holster. If spotted, I would have time for a single shot. I had no doubt that the slug would find its target, but the recoil would blow me off the cliff in the process.

A vox-caster gave a static crackle. 'Yes, my lord?' the man said, and paused for what could only be the High Duke's reply. 'Until the flames are extinguished it will be impossible to tell. Scarro and Vinka have continued to the landing pad, just in case.' Another pause. 'Of course, my lord.'

The vox static crackled again, then died. A sharp-edged flurry of gravel struck my head and shoulders, the pain of which less of an issue than the indignity.

'What's wrong with you?' the woman asked, and this time I shared her grievance. 'Do you want to stand here all night?'

There was a long silence before the man answered. I hung motionless, my fingertips and forearms burning. 'I don't know,' he said at last. 'Something feels wrong here.'

I could have told him exactly what he was sensing. I could only hope that he lacked the wit to identify the feeling for what it really was.

The woman snorted. 'Come away from the edge then, you fool.'

More gravel showered down on me as the man's footsteps receded. I let out a long, careful breath. The woman's short temper had bought me time, but the wreckage would only burn for so long. I risked another glance at the ground below, tracing the lines of the heavy metal cabling that connected the geothermal lances. They converged on a single part of the cliffside, heading into a wide-mouthed cavern directly below the fortress. That was where the power taken from Terra's heart entered the High Duke's domain. I could take the same route inside.

* * *

By the time I reached the base of the cliff my shoulders were burning and my legs shaking as though I had spent a full day on the training ground. The cavern mouth loomed ahead of me, the cables coiling around themselves like a nest of serpents as they vanished inside. I paused to catch my breath, one eye fixed on the cliff edge in case any of the High Duke's guards returned.

Why had Ceithyr decided that my death had been necessary? Surely such an astute politician must have realised Lord Malcador would hardly accept the disappearance of his agent at face value. If I had been in possession of irrefutable evidence to suggest the High Duke's guilt then I might have understood his reasoning, but I was as ignorant of his sins now – except for the attempt on my life – as I had been on my arrival. The assassination made no sense, and nor did its timing. Why wait until I was en route to my vessel when he might just as easily have dispatched me in the privacy of his own home?

It had to be something to do with the message the servant had delivered to him. That news had set off a chain of events that made my death preferable to allowing me to leave Shel'tain. But what had she told him?

My sideways scramble along the shoreline ended abruptly at the gathered conduits – vast rubberised cables banded with copper, each of them thicker than my waist – as they entered the cave mouth. There was no walkway alongside them, but looking into the depths of the cavern, I could make out a faint crimson lumen-glow. It was as I had hoped: an engineering project on this scale required access to the main building for repair and upkeep, and no one could expect the maintenance teams to arrive by the same unorthodox route that I had. My legs and shoulders still aching, I sank into the shadow of the cabling and prowled towards the light.

Inside the cavern it stank of sulphur and oil, the air full of the heat and thunder of heavy machinery. Scarlet lumens shone upwards, scattering photons into smoke and vapour and projecting the distorted shadow of a single worker onto the dripping stone walls. A narrow gantry overlooked the cavern at its innermost extent, suspended a metre and a half above the ground and accessed by a heavy metal door set securely into the stone. I found myself once again longing for my greatsword. The blade would have made short work of the heavy steel that kept me from the citadel's interior, but I had no such faith in either of my other weapons.

Once again, the lessons of the Somnus Citadel were to be my salvation. The weakness, the Matriarchs had taught us, was never in the armour, but in what it protected.

The labourer moved along the walkway behind a metal guardrail, monitoring dials, adjusting valves, sending plumes of scalding steam into the already cloudy air. As I watched, the door opened and a second man emerged, tucking something that might have been an access-wafer back into the pocket of his tunic. There it was: the weak point in the building's armour. Now I knew where to strike.

I crept forward and crouched beneath the gantry. I could see the labourers' booted feet through the cross-hatched metal, moving back and forth as they tended the machinery. Dispatching two untrained combatants would take mere moments, but if one of them triggered an emergency alarm then the situation would rapidly spiral out of control. I aimed my autopistol at the man standing above me, waited for the next discharge of steam to billow from the pipes and fired.

The slug pierced him like a lance from below, and he fell to the floor before the steam had subsided. I swung myself up and over the guardrail and stood over his corpse. The other labourer was oblivious, his attention fixed on the network of pipes and valves directly ahead of him. A second shot from my autopistol would have been the most straightforward solution, but instead I closed the distance, choosing silence over convenience. I was less than a metre away when he turned around, his expression switching from slack-jawed resignation to alarm. I silenced him with a single blow to the throat, then lowered him carefully to the floor and took his access-wafer. He was still breathing, though whether that state of affairs would continue for long was anyone's guess.

The door opened obediently in response to my newly acquired access-wafer, and I stepped into a narrow passageway that wound through a maintenance level carved deep into the rock. Power conduits and water pipes ran along the walls at ankle height. The same dull red lumens I had seen in the cavern lit the tunnel, giving the hewn stone walls an eerie, bloodstained appearance, as though I were moving through the slain carcass of a monstrous beast.

The sound of booted feet echoed down the corridor; by the sound of it, five or six guards were approaching at speed. A professionally trained agent of Lord Malcador might have chosen the path of stealth, but the instincts of a lifetime in armour ran too deep in me for that. I pressed myself back into a doorway and waited for the first of my opponents to round the corner. I caught a glimpse of a pair of wide eyes beneath an open-faced helmet and an autogun held in black-gloved hands, then ducked low, swept the legs out from under him and planted my dagger in his chest before he hit the ground.

I took the weapon from his corpse, flicked the safety catch

and aimed it at the dead man's companions. I had over-estimated their number. There were only four, counting the one bleeding his last onto my boots. I killed the second with a shot between the eyes before she had a chance to pull the trigger. The two survivors finally sprang into action, their autoguns filling the corridor with a shower of slugs, but they were too slow. One round ricocheted off my left pauldron, but I barely slowed, and the moment I reached them, the battle was over. I had the training of an Oblivion Knight, and even scorched, battered and without my sword, this was never going to be a fair fight. I kicked the barrel of the nearest guard's autogun to the side, put a round through her skull, then turned to see the last survivor wrestling furiously with the jammed mechanism of her weapon. I fired another shot, and she fell.

Four bodies. Five if I counted the labourer I had shot in the cavern, six if his companion had succumbed to his injuries. Once again, I had the nagging sense that I was the wrong person for this job. Malcador had expected subtlety and discretion, and instead I was cutting my way through the High Duke's household like a flensing knife through skin.

I took the dead guard's spare ammunition and the vox-unit from her belt. The channel was open, a frenzy of communication passing back and forth between the High Duke and his underlings. The fact of my survival was now known, and from what I was hearing, every guard in Shel'tain was converging on my position.

'Secure the nursery,' the High Duke said. Even through the crackling vox-link I could hear the urgency in his voice.

'Unas and his squad are already on their way, my lord,' a woman's voice answered.

The mention of a nursery piqued my curiosity. To the best

of my knowledge, the High Duke's progeny were long since grown, distributed across Terra as diplomatic envoys. I had seen no children during my extensive tour of the facilities, and even if there were any, what threat did Ceithyr think I posed to them?

'Go quickly,' he added, in a tone that brooked no argument. *'I will meet you there.'*

I turned off the vox-unit and spared a few seconds to check through the dead guards' ident-tags. Unas was the one I had shot in the throat, the metal disc that bore his name warm and slick with freshly spilled blood. I took his access-wafer on the assumption that his clearance would exceed that of the labourer I had robbed before, then got to my feet. This squad had been moving towards the nursery. Whoever was in there, the High Duke was adamant that I should not be allowed to reach it.

Which meant it was exactly where I intended to be.

I picked up my pace and continued in the direction the guards had been heading, past the side tunnel that led back to the generator chamber and continuing deeper into the rock, until I reached a huge set of double doors marked with the family's crow-and-longship crest. Sounds of shouting echoed down the passageway behind me. I waved Unas' access-wafer in front of the sensor on the wall. Its light flared scarlet, and with a sonorous click the door swung open.

The room inside was dark and cloyingly humid. I took a wary step across the threshold, and the door immediately slammed shut behind me. As my eyes acclimatised, I saw that the chamber was circular in shape. A greenish glow emanated from a series of water-filled glassine tanks, each one three metres in height and balanced on top of a plinth of polished black stone. Wrist-thick metal conduits connected one pillar to the next, and though the design was unfamiliar to me, I recognised the dull lustre of the stone from my days in the Somnus Citadel. The material formed part of its vast arsenal of psi-negation technology, and to find it here was deeply unsettling.

A faint, low hum vibrated through the stone floor. I moved towards the nearest of the tanks with a growing sense of unease. I raised a hand to wipe condensation from its surface, and as I did so, a humanoid shape inside recoiled from my presence, stirring the thick liquid into a froth of bubbles. Each tank contained a naked human, each in a different stage of development, ranging from a tiny sickle of flesh to a fully developed adult man.

'I knew you would come,' a young woman said.

I looked up and saw the source of the voice: a slight human figure in a plain robe standing behind a containment field that separated the main room from a shallow alcove set into the far wall. A pair of thin hands pushed back the hood, revealing watchful grey eyes set in a face with pale skin stretched over high cheekbones like a silken veil over a skull.

'What is this place?' I asked her.

'My father calls it the nursery.' Her lips curled with distaste. 'A playground for his genewrights.'

'Why does he keep you here?'

The young woman was staring at me with undisguised fascination. 'I see you with my eyes, but you are not there.'

Her reaction was astonishing. From what she was saying she had to be a psyker, but if that were the case, I would have expected her to be vomiting on the ground by now, or pressed back against the wall of her alcove to put as much distance between us as possible. She looked unsettled, but her voice stayed steady. 'I need you to trust me.'

A laugh blurted out of my throat. 'And why should I do that?'

'I have seen your futures.'

'Nonsense.' I turned my attention back to the door, straining my ears to make out the approaching footsteps. How many guards were coming? Any more than six or seven at once and I would struggle to hold them off.

'And yet it is so.' The young woman shook her head. Her hands were shaking too. The effort of will it took to stand so close to me must have been tremendous. 'You are hidden from my gifts, but I see the ripples of your passing like a stone in the river. My father' – her mouth twisted around the word – 'believes that if you leave Shel'tain alive, the family and the fortress will fall.'

'Did you send the servant to tell him that? Is that why he ordered my death?' My every instinct was screaming at me to kill the psyker, to deal with this distraction and turn my attention to the approaching enemy, but something stayed my hand. Time away from the Sisterhood was making me soft.

The footsteps reached the other side of the door, and the High Duke spoke, his voice muffled by the thick metal.

'I mean you no harm, Lady Amendera. I wish only to talk.'

I ignored him, still facing the young woman. 'If you can see the future, how do I survive this?'

The psyker pointed to a compact grey power source set into the wall. Wires from its lower edge connected the cables that ran from the granite plinths.

'Disable the psi-negation field.'

The statement was so absurd that I laughed again. 'You must think me a fool.'

The door opened. I put my back to the wall as the High

Duke strode into the room, a phalanx of guards filling the doorway behind him. A sheen of sweat stood out on his top lip, and I had the impression that his remarkable composure was close to its limits, but his hand was steady on the grip of his plasma pistol.

'Kindly drop your weapon,' he said.

I calculated the distance between us and came to an unpleasant conclusion. I could certainly get a shot off before the guards returned fire, but it would be the last thing I ever did.

'Why did you try to have me killed?' I asked instead.

The High Duke's eyes flickered to the girl behind the containment field, then back to me. 'Your fate and that of my family are intimately intertwined. I received word from my seer that if you are allowed to leave this place, my house will fall.'

'So you decided that killing an agent of Lord Malcador was preferable?'

'A hasty decision, I grant you.' The High Duke smiled. 'And yet that decision has served only to highlight your impressive skills. A woman of your aptitude and experience would be welcome as part of my household. We have profited greatly from the psykers our genewrights have engineered from the family bloodline over the last few decades. With their foreknowledge, the strings of fate can be pulled in our favour. I can see no reason why you would not also thrive here.'

I stared at him, trying to untangle the meaning from his flowery words. Was he offering me a job?

'My service is already pledged,' I said.

'Indeed.' The High Duke spoke calmly, as though we were meeting over drinks in his parlour instead of in a genewright's horror-filled laboratory. 'Pledged to a man who fails to appreciate your unique gifts. You are a warrior to the core, Lady Amendera. To attempt to reforge a master-crafted weapon such as yourself is a travesty. As head of my household guard in Shel'tain, you would live a life of comfort, accorded status befitting your skills.'

I gave myself a moment to consider. I had no reason to trust the High Duke, but the prospect of continued existence did seem preferable to death by plasma. More than that, he was offering me a return to a simpler life, one where my sole duty would be to fight and kill on command. Shel'tain would be my prison, but it would be a gilded one.

'And if I refuse?' I said, wondering if I sounded as uncertain as I felt. 'What will you tell Lord Malcador, or the next agent he sends to investigate my disappearance?'

He gave an elegant one-shouldered shrug. 'I will have the currents of fate examined once again and choose the path that promises the best of all possible futures for my family.'

'Your family.' I gestured to the tanks and their unnatural contents. 'Like these wretches?'

The High Duke laughed, a derisive sound with no mirth or warmth. 'These? They might share my blood, but that hardly makes them human.'

'You cannot let him do this!' the young woman behind the containment field shouted. I turned and saw genuine panic on her face, her eyes locked on to mine with desperate intensity. 'You cannot trust him. All of this is his doing – the experiments, the failed attempts. I have seen it all.'

The High Duke ignored her. 'You yourself were made to hunt these mutants, Lady Amendera. I simply wish to put them to profitable use, for the good of my family and the Imperium.'

'Very well,' I said, and the High Duke's face widened into a beaming smile.

'A wise decision.'

I stooped and placed the autogun on the ground. The girl behind me gave a long, drawn-out wail of despair.

'I commend you on your foresight,' the High Duke said.

In one smooth movement, I rose to my feet and hurled my dagger into the module that connected the stone plinths. There was a dull implosion, then sparks showered into air that stank of ozone as the lights went out. I threw myself into the shadow behind the closest of the tanks. The hum of the psi-negators ceased, and the reaction from the psykers inside the chambers was instantaneous, the room filling with the sound of limbs slamming against glass.

'This is how it ends,' the young woman said.

'Liar!' the High Duke growled. Lumen-beams mounted to his guards' weapons pierced the darkness like spotlights. 'You are a seer, mutant, nothing more. How can you hope to–'

The tank nearest the door erupted in a fountain of synthetic amnion and broken glass. Slugs tore through the air as the psyker inside slithered to the ground, but they bounced harmlessly away as though stopped by an invisible force field.

'Kill them all!' the High Duke howled, then his voice was abruptly silenced. One moment he had been a living, breathing man, the next he was a crumpled sphere of raw meat and jagged bone ends that hung for an instant in the air before falling wetly to the ground. The psyker from the tank raised a gel-slick hand and sent the first rank of guards flying backwards. They hit the walls of the passageway hard enough that I heard bones rupture, followed by a series of crunches and squelches as they suffered the same fate as their master.

The room fell silent. I lit my own lumen, recovered my autogun and pointed it at the psyker's head. The man made no effort to move. Blood was seeping from his eyes and nose, mixing with the thick fluid that clung to his skin. Pink froth bubbled on his lips with each laboured gasp. He was dying.

'I could hear him,' the girl said. 'My brother. All this time I could hear him in my head. The pain he was in. How much he wanted to die.'

The psyker's eyes fixed upon mine, his breathing becoming slower and more ragged. The power he had displayed was terrifying, even more so when I considered that I was mere metres away from him. If the High Duke had been allowed to breed more monstrosities such as this, the risk to the Imperium would have been unimaginable. I waited until he had breathed his last before I looked away.

The room stank like a charnel house. I had a sudden urge for clean air, but I had one more matter to attend to before I could leave.

'Don't,' the girl said, before I turned. 'Please...'

Her hands reached out to me, her grey eyes beseeching. The sight would have been a pitiful one, if there had been any pity left in me. Years of training and every instinct in my body urged me to kill her. Despite being an unwilling slave she was the key to the High Duke's schemes, and turning on her master at the last did nothing to atone for her past. Everything I knew told me that the only mercy I owed her was a quick death.

'Please,' she said again. 'I can be useful to you.'

I beckoned her forward, but she didn't move. She was like an animal at bay, unsure of whether it was an invitation to freedom or to death, and in truth I had not yet decided. She may indeed prove useful to our cause, but I could already see the look of disgust on my fellow agents' faces and hear the superstitious whisperings of the adepts and attendants in Lord Malcador's service were I to return with a psyker in tow. She would bring ill fortune, turn fate against us, interfere with our great work and the manifest destiny of humankind.

But it was that thought, more than anything else, that led me to spare her. Superstition and fear of the unknown may well be etched deep into the heart of humanity, but they were no basis for rational decision-making. And if what the girl said was true? If she really could see the branching strands of the future like streams of running water, then she would be of immeasurable use to me in my service to Lord Malcador and the Throne. I hoped my patron would agree.

'Do you have a name?' I said, turning away before she answered. The sound of delicate footsteps told me that she was following me.

'He never gave me one,' she replied.

She stopped to take one last look at the restless figures in their glass prisons. 'What will happen to the others?' she asked.

'That will be for Lord Malcador to decide,' I told her.

Their fate, like mine, lay in his hands.

YOUR NEXT READ

HORUS RISING
by Dan Abnett

After thousands of years of expansion and conquest, the human Imperium is at its height. His dream for humanity accomplished, the Emperor hands over the reins of power to his Warmaster, Horus, and heads back to Terra.

PAIN ENGINE

CHRIS THURSTEN

The path begins at the Feast of Keening Razors.

The brutalities and death games of the arena followed a pattern of escalation – lethal competition orchestrated with an artist's eye and an epicure's palate. Terrorised alien captives were harried into the path of scything Hellions; these same were then dragged to the ground by the impossible acrobatics of the wyches of the Razor. My archon, Torakhis, bade his Trueborn forward and then halted the order, his attention arrested by the weapon brought forth by his rival, Raidmaster Nahaerian.

Her contribution to the Feast was a single combatant – a Pain Engine, hunchbacked and barbed, whose glowering aspect drew all eyes inward. It was a singular thing, redolent with suffering, and though it is rare for a haemonculus to acknowledge the mastery of another's work, I did so. Nahaerian's herald stepped forward atop her twin-decked barge and projected a single word:

SEETHE.

The gathered throng erupted and the fray that followed was a paean to violence. My archon shuddered at the affront of it, but he could not deny the Engine's potency and nor could I. To the craftless, this was a single moment of overwhelming ecstasy. To me, it was but a crack of light through a doorway. The path began at the Feast of Keening Razors, and I felt all the joy and agony of fate diverted.

Now, centuries later, I feel nothing.

I descend the final step and face a wall engraved with the master's sigil. Aside from that jagged mark, its surface is smooth and flat, a slab of dark metal that pinches across the twisting pathway like a suture.

Why do I not sense it?

This is a lost, lightless place, a cavity scarcely fit to die in. Yet it is the privilege of the haemonculus to curate sensation beyond such mundanity, to trace the unseen patterns of a murderous universe and bend them to new purpose. A teeming array of sensor-grafts and spliced nerves blossom upon my palms and I direct them to the sigil – and then beyond, to an orbital ridge, molecule-thin, that indicates the presence of a hidden aperture.

Where is the agony that made thralls of Halfborn and archons alike?

My senses bared, I strain beyond the portal for the soul-scent of the Pain Engine called Seethe, whose secrets I have pursued across a graveyard's fill of lifetimes. Nothing.

Yet.

I know that I am upon the final threshold. Knowledge, cruelly won, has permitted me to undertake this last journey into the black depths of Commorragh. At every step, a tithe has been levied – and I have spent lavishly, goading my followers forward into the myriad horrors that protect the hidden paths of the haemonculi. This is, after all, the expense for which they were spared.

It has gratified me, in the course of the descent, to elevate this grim transaction to poetry. When a flesh-crafted terror uncoiled itself from its dank eyrie and set about us, starved and soul-mad, I bade my kabalites to hand their weapons to the menials in my service and withdraw. We slipped away under the cover of howls and splinter-fire, the shriek of blades drawn in darkness, the struggle and shock of death-in-shadow. I drank the kabalites' disquiet as something like martial privilege was granted to the lowest among us at their expense.

The loss of their armaments unsettled them, and I sensed the cracks in their resolve as they returned to their posts at the vanguard of our expedition. There, the bitterness of their obligation to me was slowly replaced by thoughts of an archon's favour upon their return. Uneasy minds peered out beyond the darkness of the path and quieted themselves with dreams of the raids to come. They heard the shuddering wail of skimmer engines, felt the kick of a new rifle, inhaled blood and pain under bright, burning skies.

My kabalites did not feel the soft press of armoured boots upon a bed of swollen little bulbs, nor did they taste the shimmer in the air. We watched as they blundered duty-blind into the perils of the master's garden, then we diverted our path and left them foetal in the darkness, lost to creeping fantasia, fallen irrecoverably from the ladders of power.

As for my acolytes, those who would shadow me on the master's path – for these bright ones I reserved the most ignoble ends. I let the gleam of ambition linger in their eyes long enough to see it bisected by red lines of sprung monofilament. I heard the unspoken treacheries on their breath as it was crushed from them under the weight of crudely set rockfalls. I waited long seconds when the ground gave way beneath them, and I let the squalid report of their terminal descent stand as the final word on aspiration.

It is in this way that I have made the path my own, taken the snares set to slay me and incorporated them into my own art. It is the fatal error of students to assume that these final steps lead to the master – they must be taken as the master or they must not be taken at all. As I near the hidden domain of Seethe's creator, I do so alone, in the creator's stolen image.

I drift closer to the doorway, sensors at high baud, alert to threat. Nothing. Null. The walls are thick and sense-dead. The master's chamber could draw power from the effluent of the blazing Ilmaea and I would not know it.

Perhaps this is also why I do not sense the Pain Engine. Its power marked me, I acknowledge, as it hung low and heavy over the fighting pit. A brute weapon should not radiate such delicate grief, nor such ruinous ecstasy. We each felt it – the ravenous Halfborn pressing to the arena's edge, the Heketarii dying upon the blood-thick sands, the archon at my side. The shock of Seethe's potency slipped through layers of vicious self-government and spoke something to my soul. My ingress to its creator's domain is a gesture returned.

I extend a grafted anterior limb to the sigil and push. I permit the stolen flesh some autonomy for a moment, allowing its subdued nerves to flare to life, alert not just to the possibility of death but the myriad forms that death might take – the acid heat of a disintegration charge, the tang of a concealed blade, the hard-coursing blood of a lurking assassin.

Nothing. The door communicates only the weariness of old metal. It yields. It is open.

Pale light casts up from an aperture in the centre of a round chamber whose upper reaches are lost to darkness. Curving workbenches of the same dark metal are arrayed around the room's circumference, and each subsequent step requires me to navigate a hanging knot of hooked chains or a mess of razorwire nets laden with tools and grisly biomatter.

At the heart of these descending hazards hangs the carapace of a Pain Engine. My heart – my Trueborn heart – beats, but it is not Seethe. Its arching shell is empty, and no life animates the long synthetic nerve-links that hang low alongside its dangling blade-mounts.

I am familiar with such assemblies. I have brought them to shrieking animation many times. I understand that the shell of this Pain Engine is a starting point – a common element that binds me to its creator, a blank canvas on which to paint the secrets of Seethe. In its low-hung aspect, softly lit by the aperture below, I perceive something else – an invitation.

The intent of the workshop's architect is latent in the radial arrangement of the space, in the breadth and specificity of its stores of grim detritus. Yet this is more than static symbolism – I perceive the presence of an attentive mind. Drukhari have long since stepped away from the path of seers, but we remain as alert to sign and posture as any of our kind. More so, in fact, as our methods of expression are neither masked by sardonic pomposity nor cauterised by self-denial.

There is grandeur in us, and there is grandeur in this moment. I comprehend that my long pursuit is at an end. Seethe's creator, its nameless master, is here. What remains is negotiation, resolution and conclusion – by necessity a mutual process, albeit one that I alone intend to survive. I speak.

'Hidden one. I sense your eyes upon me.'

Silence and stillness for a long moment. Then a voice, rendered grating and discordant by crude electronic transmission.

'Aspirant.'

The word strikes at me from a point in the darkness a few degrees from the flank of the hanging shell. My senses twist to face it.

'Nadirist aspect, split by scarlet. Apothist rising.'

The voice is unnatural, and then I catch the reason – its waning resonance lingers around a rudimentary transmission system that hangs from the neck of an alien slave. The device is stamped with crude winged insignia, as is a taut and mortifying section of the corpse's scalp. Its output hangs low around the creature's disembowelled navel. Their remaining organs are dark, hard, desiccated things, indistinct from the crude equipment that their owner once dragged from world to starving world.

'Covenless. Craft-mongrel.'

I drift a step towards the voice, bearing all of my attention down upon it, driving my inviolable form towards the source of these crass descriptors. Then I feel the intelligence that drives them evading me. A susurrus of whispers sweeps around to my rear. I turn a little too swiftly, betraying impatience.

'A game, then,' I reply. 'Our exchange is to take the form of a game.'

'Postulator.'

This time the voice is rich, Commorrite, and resonates from the gilded mask of a Scourge. Her wings are missing but she hangs from chains as if arrested in flight. Her gaze is fixed and keen, and I feel for a fleeting moment the sting of interpersonal connection. The moment passes. This is necrochemical puppetry and trivial electroprojection, nothing more.

I cease moving and adopt a high posture that states, *Elude and surround me. I welcome it. In doing so, you confirm my centrality.*

'I do not make assumptions,' I say with lilting certainty. 'You desire further tests, further tricks. This evasive display is unbecoming, and a disappointment.' I hazard a low blow. 'Perhaps I am in the wrong place.'

A desiccated ur-ghul twitches violently at my feet, rasping as its wide maw forms unfamiliar sounds.

'Error prone.'

I allow the returned insult to pass in a long moment. Stillness and quiet return, broken only by the soft hiss of my elongated spine as it coils and uncoils beneath me. I dim my senses as if in repose – and then with detached precision I impel the bladed tip of my spine up through the roof of the ur-ghul's mouth, rending dry muscle and brittle bone as I make a dangling marionette of the wretched thing. A hard twist severs the neck; I allow the body to collapse to the workshop floor and withdraw the cranium into the folds of my garments. I have no use for it, but this subtraction from the master's stock is necessary. I wish us to remain in the domain of tithes and transactions.

The voice offers no response. This is not unexpected, but it is undesirable. As I shift closer to the shell of the Pain Engine, I re-engage my senses and grant it my full attention. I make a show of it – palms forward, body twisting, head raised, focus narrowing to a single point at the expense of my broader awareness. It is an act of courteous dominance:

Let us return to matters of mutual interest, wedded to *After all, you cannot hurt me.*

When the master next speaks, it is from a new source, close by the Engine itself.

'Seethe-seeker.'

'At last,' I reply, smiling, 'a truth passes between us.'

The voice now emanates from a decrepit collection of drukhari heads hanging not far from the Engine's faceplate. These unfortunates have been flayed and acid-fused to the bulbous tip of a dark armature. Its articulated body nestles among hanging ephemera of no great value, but close inspection reveals a significant and singular piece of machinery. A favoured tool.

'You truly will not face me, then,' I say with a sigh. 'Do you fear a confrontation?'

'Fear is an element of the work.'

This response comes from another face, fixed to the same device. I tilt my head and hold my smile. *Ah, there you are.*

'As a measure of success? Yes. In an artisan of your alleged calibre? I find it unbecoming.'

'This has been stated.'

'Am I incorrect?'

The pattern changes – the voice shifts back to the previous speaker, the first face to address me. It is truly decrepit, but there is Trueborn dignity in its deep-lined features. It speaks conversationally, in a familiar register.

'You speak of becoming and unbecoming. I become nothing. I am the voice of the work. Nothing more.'

'Nothing more.' I make a show of deliberation, pausing to test the words. 'Very well. What price does the *work* demand?'

We are drukhari. To us, nothing is nothing.

'An articulation of understanding,' says one voice.

'An interrogation of the journey undertaken,' adds another.

The armature twitches – a sudden, fractional motion, a hypnic spasm as its animating intelligence darts to a third location. 'A catalogue of shapes adopted.'

'I see,' I reply. 'I understand.'

Here is a barbed incongruence. A trial of this kind is a means of winnowing pretenders, not drawing something of value from a master. Every haemonculus of worth understands this, because every haemonculus of worth has survived it. Indeed, the version of myself who first learned to twist such tests to their own benefit resides in a deep and beloved part of my memory. As I call upon their skills, I walk with them through the hallways of my first youth, sharing the vertiginous potential of natural genius. The hidden master wishes to walk this territory with me? I welcome them.

'A catalogue of shapes?' I say, affecting amusement. 'I favour this articulation. True craft, I have found, calls for a degree of... division.' I pause on the final word.

You are in my domain now.

'Division is essential to the orderly arrangement of one's faculties, unhindered by debts or allegiances – to an Overlord, to a coven or to the Muses themselves.'

I position myself closer to the heart of the chamber, savouring the pleasures of spoken apostasy. My gaze returns to the faces upon the armature. 'I'm sure you understand,' I add with a smile.

I define truth within my borders.

'You called me craft-mongrel. That was a test. You attempted to goad me into denying the simple truth that binds us here, which is that we ply the unalloyed truths of the fleshcrafter's art. We hone our scalpels upon fundamental shapes.'

The fingers on my rightmost hand uncurl as I unsheathe

three surgical talons. Red ichor seethes and settles around punctured fingertips. I present the blades to the room, letting them quiver in the upcast light. 'Three truths, I think, will do for our purposes,' I say. 'I offer you truths of flesh, of blood and of bone.'

There is a prolonged pause, undercut by the feeling of something shifting in the darkness. Close by my ear, a honeyed whisper from the dead Scourge.

'Continue.'

I return to the Feast of Keening Razors, the first touch, and the onset of the work.

By the time my skimmer set down upon the arena sands, the Pain Engine was already gone, escorted from the field by the personal guard of Archon Nahaerian, her point made. I noted the brand of my patron, Archon Torakhis, on the flesh of the scavenger wracks that set about reclaiming worthy material from the day's maimed and slain. The fleshcrafter Vyst passed among them, stooped like a menial. The sight of him prompted no surprise – Vyst was a pit-butcher first and foremost, a haemonculus only by basest technicality.

Even so, I recognised the significance of his movements. He drifted among the recently slain, seeking those overcome by Seethe. I watched him dart to the side of a mauled wych, her body scoured with chain-flail lacerations, and begin a hurried flensing that left him bent and blood-slick. When he rose from his work and his eyes met mine, I knew that he had seen what I had seen. Though I did not desire it, a covenant formed between us – long before words were exchanged, and longer still before Torakhis committed us, in his acrimonious way, to the task of replicating Nahaerian's prized weapon.

Only much later would I determine that the secrets of the

Pain Engine lay with the creator, not the work. For a time, however, Vyst's methods were of use to me. He made obsessive study of the wounds inflicted by Seethe and sought the means to replicate them. He convinced Torakhis to underwrite the revivification of the Pain Engine's victims and pitted them against contraptions of his own design.

A great expense was levied in order to learn that expense alone was not enough to achieve our aims – a useful lesson, albeit one of greater value to me than it was to Vyst, who had ordered the tests and expended his archon's favour in doing so. When a particularly dangerous Heketarii bested one of Vyst's creations and escaped, red-eyed and soul-frenzied, his collar was tightened – to my benefit.

A portion of the fleshcrafter's workshops were reassigned for my use, and with them the greater portion of his stock of flesh. This penalty should have made Vyst more cautious, but instead he writhed with the shame of it. I goaded him further by feigning progress, though I now knew his methods to be of limited use. Vyst's rage was a wound that granted me access to the red meat of his psyche, and by inches I carved the notion that our archon's tight fist was the sole cause of his failure.

Vyst incurred deep debts with slavers and alien flesh-tenders as he sought to restore what he believed to be his. When progress was unforthcoming, he grew desperate. Oaths were undertaken that no loyal servant should undertake, and threads of foreign influence were woven into the spire's foundations by the needle of Vyst's obsession.

Torakhis' usurpation was swift and, to bitter and distracted Vyst, a lethal surprise. A descendant scented weakness and struck; for a night, the spire came alive with darklight and dissembly. Archon Aekaris was a shrewd successor, and it was a small thing to provoke disdain for the vain preoccupations of the recently deposed. At a stroke the remainder of Vyst's holdings were mine, among them the agonised and phage-twisted remains of the pit-butcher himself.

I made lavish use of Vyst's revivification arrays in the centuries that followed, although something of the flesh-crafter's soul was lost with each subsequent reanimation. His debt-holders were repaid with a wealth of heedless, vat-cloned simulacra, and my own studies never suffered for want of bodies. When Vyst's soul finally wore too thin to bear further replication, I embodied what remained in a quivering grotesque. The creature had few uses but served as a reminder of the pain-scent of Seethe, something so singular that no amount of debasement could erase it. I named him Spoor, this broken companion, and he would remain by my side for many lifetimes. His value finally revealed itself amidst the horrors of the master's menagerie, in the darkness of the final path, and his last words were a howl of devotion as, armed with a kabalite's borrowed knife, he loped away to meet death on my behalf.

Vyst was there at the beginning, Spoor at the end. Almost.

'Flesh is currency,' I say, withdrawing a talon. I make a show of ruminatory distraction, considering the stitchwork of my garments, settling my gaze upon a leather cuff whose inner lining still carries something of Vyst's original pallor. 'To be debased, and exalted, as we see fit.'

There is silence, followed by the click of an unseen mechanism. I sense the affirmation in it and proceed.

'Let us speak of blood.'

My memory alights upon a time of change, of bonds exchanged, the re-articulation of the path.

The mind of Archon Aekaris was ever fixed on high-spire

politicking, on the favour games and lethal innuendos that burn ever brighter in ambitious minds as one draws closer to the Supreme Overlord's radiant sphere. When the wealth of the kabal ceased to propel my research, I made a bid for independence. It was granted with the flick of a wrist. Aekaris declined to face me, their gaze fixed hard on the city, body turned to the light of the Ilmaea, taut and hungry like a barbwrack vine. I suspected then that I was being granted a spore's freedom, sensed that the archon understood that whatever fertility I enjoyed in my independence would eventually feed their power base. This suspicion was confirmed when, upon my departure, a skimmer craft and a full complement of kabalites were rededicated to my service.

I did not reject the gesture. At my direction, the skimmer dived precipitously from the spire and levelled out on the periphery of Sec Maegra. We registered only briefly on the scanners of Low Commorragh as we darted swiftly towards the Bone Middens, our souls and sensors frayed by the proximity of gloaming Aelindrach. Thus I took my adopted band of preening Halfborn and thrust them into the domain of wyches and outcasts.

No cruelty is without purpose. Among the lesser cults and avaricious menagerists of this low domain there was a diversity of form and experience absent elsewhere. I substituted the well-kept blade for the rusted knife and found pleasure in this unsanitary place, in the immediacy of its lusts and manias.

Years passed in profitable malefaction, and in dextrous service to the cults, before fate returned me to the path. A gout of red lightning spat a burning Raider into the heart of the Middens, its descent levelling a boulevard of ossified statuary. A sole survivor emerged – the Nemesine Talec, pain-master to the Archite Karasikh, huntress of the Scirocco Fray, once pledged to the great Raidmaster Nahaerian. Patron of Seethe.

The unmistakable soul-mark of the Pain Engine was upon her. I sensed it immediately, Spoor howling and jittering by my side. The Nemesine looked upon me and sensed it also. Our paths converged and began to flow together.

To Talec, the Nemesine path did not conclude with absolute command of the killing art. She was a practitioner also, possessed of a pragmatism honed by long years in realspace, and this granted her a compelling ease among the denizens of the Middens. I would have found this unseemly were it not evidently the device of a sharp mind, and I would have baulked at an alliance – at the notion of our equality – were it not for Talec's extended exposure to Seethe. She boasted of trailing the Pain Engine in a swift skimmer, of being called to acts of savagery in its pursuit, of the blood art she rendered in its wake.

The Bone Middens were fertile ground for stories such as these. For the first time I faced the prospect of meaningful assistance in the furtherance of my ambitions, and our bond was the seed from which a movement grew. A new coven is a fragile thing, both delicate and defiant by nature, but we were strangers to neither danger nor apostasy.

Talec and I enjoyed dyadic authority, turning our divergent aspects to the harvest of secrets from the seekers drawn into our orbit. A few of them bore the scent of the Engine, and by increments the existence of the hidden master became known to us. It was a scant thing – a shape that framed an absence – but it meant progress, and it meant power.

Power shared.

I did not give voice to my agitation, but nor did I attempt to hide it. Talec, for her part, displayed no concern. Her craft began to transcend Nemesine preoccupations with the termination of life and grew into a study of that which remains. She dwelled upon entrail truths and blood patterns, and in these she claimed to identify something fundamental to Seethe's signature – a scream in rondel, a cyclic pattern that begat itself, blood calling for blood.

I grew uneasy at the composure that this understanding appeared to grant her, but soon understood that what I truly objected to was the weakness that it implied. In the final hours of our partnership, she bade me join her to assess the aftermath of a conflict between two of our acolytes. They had turned on one another over a praxic disagreement and set to mutual butchery. As Talec turned to consider the grisly display, her arms raised in amusement, I erased her swiftly with an underslung destructor that I had carried since the day of our first meeting. I acid-purged every part of the Nemesine Talec, blood and legacy both, until I could be sure that the timeless city would forget her completely.

What Commorragh has lost, I have retained. The Nemesine's voice circulates in me even now.

The second talon is withdrawn. 'Blood is a messenger,' I say aloud. 'A universal language. A binding medium.'

I am brushed by attentive whispers. I feel the apprehension in it and catch this fresh recognition before it can flee.

'Of course,' I add, 'sometimes a stain is just a stain.'

Two long heartbeats. Eyes upon me. *There must be a response.*

Motion. The armature shudders, presenting a new speaker.

'After flesh, after blood…'

'Bone,' I eagerly respond.

I feel myself flush with natural adrenaline. *I am so close.* I allow the assembly of auxiliary spines that emerge from my back to fan apart and shudder in a predator's display.

I return to the coven, to jealous winnowings and bloody consolidation.

The seeker Sziadan arrived upon our shared path having exhausted the deepest pain-lore of nine lesser covens. They sought the truth of Seethe with a razor intellect and a cynicism born of long-delayed gratification. An ascetic by the standards of our kind, they lingered at the periphery of our hidden band, solemn, speaking their secrets only to Talec and then, in her absence, to no one.

I defiled their solemnity with a toxin that whispered red murder to their marrow.

The vital reagent originated on a maiden world whose people possessed a primitive understanding of the relationship between the Bonesinger's art and simple fungal parasitism. There, a particular bulb had catalysed great acts of ancestor worship over the course of slow millennia. That world had since burned at the whim of lesser races, her people swept aside as peripheral casualties of an irrelevant war. My personal stock was hence acquired from a corsair, a newcomer to Commorragh flush with the confidence particular to free aeldari, gutted with a long knife in an alley off the slave docks at the bottom of Corespur.

It was the work of days to render the toxin, weeks to draw close enough to Sziadan to permit its application. Mere hours for its transformative work to begin. Sziadan's soul was drawn inwards, severed from their bodily gestalt and bound to the fundamental ache, the deep-clawing nerve-mania of their own bones. At the culmination of the infection, Sziadan's now-conscious skeletal structure tore its way loose and savaged a number of our shared assistants before being cut down in turn.

An indelicate end, an act of tribute. A libation for the Dark City upon the eve of departure.

I venture another step closer to the hanging shell, emboldened, reaching a long Trueborn arm up into the mass of hooked chains that hold the Engine's blade-mount in place. A firm pull and the device is free, though not without cost – a stray hook rips a jagged tear in my forearm. I thrill at it. I am committed. A sharp vial of countertoxin presses into my back. I raise my gaze and present the empty blade-mount.

'Bone is a weapon,' I say. 'The hard core of violence inherent to the living. It falls to us to unsheathe it.'

I luxuriate in Sziadan, in their shrieking rebirth, in the blood and terror of their brief second life, in the shearing and snapping agony of their second death, in the residual soul-ache that lingers in the auxiliary spine that twitches above my shoulder. I revel in all of the voices I carry with me, in the profane geometries of betrayal, in the artistry with which I am remade.

I have arrived at the chamber's centre. I am exultant, garbed in grisly capital, dripping a red manifesto to the chamber floor, purified by violence. My soul presses in upon the moment, insistent, imminent like gravity. Here at the end of the path is a final argument: *I am singular and you will yield to me.*

There is no response.

It is an unbearable insult to lavish such attention upon a machine. My senses race to the chamber's periphery, skittering against the cold rock for a sign of the alcove where the master must have secreted themselves. My soul-potency goes with them, blossoming as I embrace my own totality. There is danger in this. I am split, both cocoon and emergent creature, yet each form feels the dread attention fall upon it, the whisper upon the neck, the thirsting claw that rakes the mirror – but what of it?

I am singular.

You will yield to me.

'Aspirant approved. Organic matter accepted for Engine-meld.'

The words are spoken in a dead register. I recoil at their leaden mundanity, which hangs in the air for a moment like a handful of stones cast in the path of divinity. As their resonance fades, my eminence curdles to wrath, even as a distracted spar of my intelligence wonders at something dreadful: *Stones have gravity, too.*

I feel the predator at my back withdraw as exultance gives way to fury and violence comes quicker than thought. I draw my destructor and raze the head of the armature, searing its dead faces to vapour and exposing the metal beneath. Something guttural escapes me as the acid completes its corrosive work. Then fury returns: I sweep the weapon in a swift orbit, casting its beam towards the ceiling. I compose myself amidst the chaos of tumbling equipment and rent razorwire.

Yet the destruction of the master's chamber cannot alter a course whose purpose is only now understood. Neither wrath nor terror has the power to neutralise the corrosive truth to which I am exposed, the acid recursion of Seethe. I am drawn back to the Feast of Keening Razors, feeling myself hang low and heavy over the fighting pit, radiating the same grief and ecstasy that I now struggle in vain to contain.

'Soul-drift within tolerances. Scarlet abiding.'

These words barely register above the undignified collapse of the workshop's stores of grisly material. Only a few voices remain.

'Nadirist rising. Apothist rising. Division-rune ignition.'

A single whispering source, now. Above, within the Engine.

'The work concludes.'

Behind me, the entrance to the master's domain yawns wide. Through it lies an outbound journey that culminates in Commorragh, in new lives and new paths to power. Above me, in the shell, a darker passage opens. I do not require nerve-grafted sensors or darting ocular arrays to locate it. I feel it. I felt it in the moment that goaded elation gave way to rage, in the desolation that has followed the subversion of my pride.

The domain of tithes has collapsed, and what remains is an unnavigable ultimatum – a twist of paradox like the jaws of a snare. To take the outbound path is to concede failure, to refuse to complete the work, to defy the master's assessment and declare myself insufficient. To complete the work, however, is to accept terminal bondage. I perceive now what Talec understood – the endless curvature of the inbound path, whose final form is an unbreakable knot of strife.

I locate the mark of Seethe within myself and regard it with detached admiration. It is a singular reagent, difficult to procure, the end product of a process like alchemy, whose elements must be held in the most delicate balance for an unthinkable amount of time. I recoil at the taste of my own soul, recognising a richness born of slow and deliberate fermentation.

I rise upon my coiling spine. The shell draws me in, and I am greeted in love and agony by a thousand flensing barbs.

The work begins. *There is nothing else.*

YOUR NEXT READ

GOTHGHUL HOLLOW
by Anna Stephens

The once illustrious Gothghul family endures seasons of isolation in their castle overlooking the Hollow. But when the town is threatened by a spate of sinister manifestations, they must uncover a diabolic mystery to which they have but one clue: Mhurghast.

CHAINS

JONATHAN D BEER

Rakove looms over her, impassively watching her struggle as the gas fills her narrow prison.

It is not pride that drives her to fight, because she has never known the luxury of pride. The privilege of dignity. Nor is she trying to free herself – she's learnt that the tough synthweave cuffs are beyond her malnourished strength. And a part of her welcomes the relief that the gas brings. The shrieking cacophony of other people's thoughts only abates when her gaolers render her unconscious. She fights just as hard when they wake her, fingers scraping at the transparent interior of her coffin cage in a desperate attempt to claw her way back to the peace of narcotic-induced slumber.

No, she fights as a chained animal fights, and for the same reason. Her limbs thrash against the bonds that encircle her wrists and ankles, that press tight against her chest and forehead. She spits and hisses, screaming the curses she's learnt as a vagrant thief of Varangantua's pitiless streets. She even tries to lash out with her witch sense, imagining her body's pain as a dagger that she hurls at Rakove's inscrutable form. But she has never really controlled the power that afflicts her, and if her mind's blade lands, he shows no sign of feeling it.

The agony collar bites, its barbs flooding her veins with punishment for her pointless resistance. Her body arcs, muscles locked with pain, tears streaming from her eyes.

Finally, she slumps against the coffin's bare steel, though the collar continues to scourge her. She has had the strength to fight stolen by the gas that hisses from inlets beside her head and must now endure in mute misery.

As the soporific takes hold, Rakove continues to watch her. She looks back at him through the thick plex, his fleshy face turned into smears of colour by the curve of the coffin's lid. Desperation drives her to plead, though she knows there's nothing she can say that will lead him to free her. She can feel his thoughts, hot and cruel behind bloodshot eyes. There is no compassion in him, not for her.

Only contempt.

Melita lurched out of her chair, flailing at the phantom sensation of cuffs on her wrists and fire blazing through her limbs. She scraped her hip against her metal desk's hard edge as she stood, yelped and staggered away. An errant step caught a pile of paper and data-wafers, spilling them in a rippling cascade across the office floor.

She stood in the centre of the room, chest heaving, fists balled. It was dark, and though Melita wanted to snap the lumens on, she couldn't make herself move. She forced in one breath after another, reaching for calm even as her heart thundered. She swore, shuddered and swore again. Each curse was jarringly loud in the near silence, but they helped her shed the cloying, aching touch of the memory that was not hers.

It had been the sound of her cogitators this time. For a moment, the rhythm of valves switching, the hum-click of magnetic coils engaging and disengaging within the steel and brass bowels of the machinery that crowded the room's far wall, had synchronised into the same warbling pattern as the engines that had pumped the soporific gas into her cage.

No. Into Alim's cage. Not hers. It had been the boy who had endured that torture, not Melita.

All at once, the tension left her body, taking her strength with it. Melita collapsed back into her chair, grateful as ever for the embrace of its cracked, welcoming synthleather. As it always did, a headache had begun to bloom behind her eyes, sharp and bitter as the memory that had assailed her. She swore once more and put her head in her hands.

A pale finger strayed to the skin of her throat, remembering the barbs of the hateful collar. The sight of red weals around Alim's neck from their punishment. That had been how Melita had found him, chained and caged by the cruel cabal who had been using him for his unnatural powers.

Melita sighed, guilt and anger adding their sour edge to her throbbing headache. She had saved the boy from their clutches, and, in return, Alim – that was the only name he had given her, and despite furious research she had been unable to uncover any record of the boy's existence – had used his unnatural abilities to thrust his memories into her mind.

That was how the mutant psyker had forced her to shoot him. He had begged for it, pleaded for the las-bolt that would put an end to his misery. She had only pulled the trigger to stem the awful tide of pain and indignity that he had violently shared with her.

But they had stayed with her. Even after two months, the

memories were as vivid as ever, triggered by stray sights, sounds or scents. Three days ago, she had nearly bolted from a meeting with one of her informants. A juve had rounded the street corner tossing a handball from palm to palm. Instantly, she had lapsed, overcome by the recollection of sudden shock and pain as a rock struck Alim's scalp. The jeers and curses of the encircling crowd. It had taken all her self-control not to set off running, driven by survival instincts from another person's life.

Melita uncovered her eyes and kicked her chair into a slow spin to take her back to face her desk.

More data-wafers and folders littered its surface. One – the only one that mattered – sat beside her primary runeboard, caught in a pool of yellow light from her desk-lumen.

A face glared at her from a pict fixed to the cover, hard eyes almost lost amid puffy features and a cobweb of broken veins. The image was from Jorg Rakove's service record, taken just a few years before he retired from the enforcers. There were others inside the folder, pulled from the data archives of joy house monitor picters and district Administratum residency records, and even a still from a propaganda reel in which he'd featured some thirty years ago as a young sanctioner. They sat alongside a detailed biography, constructed over weeks of arduous research. Melita had traced the path of Rakove's life, learning all she could about Alim's tormentor as she hunted him.

The man had gone to ground, hiding from the justice he deserved. The Valtteri Cartel – Melita's new employers – had tasked her with running him down. Rakove was the only link to whoever had orchestrated Alim's capture and the attacks that had brought the all-powerful alliance of merchant-combines to the brink of civil war. Such elaborate hostility could not be ignored, and Melita had been given access to a seemingly bottomless well of slate with which to pursue him. She doubted there was a single snitch or ganger from Dragosyl to Setomir who didn't know Rakove's face.

It was the Valtteri's wrath that Rakove ran from, but it had been Melita's need for vengeance that had driven her through the long nights at her cogitators. She doubted Rakove had ever heard her name, but she knew him, intimately, and not merely from her assembled notes. Alim had been his captive for weeks. The boy had known the taste of Rakove's thoughts, and he had forced that on her along with so much else.

Melita stared at the pict, meeting the sanctioner-turned-torturer's gaze. Revulsion and rage churned within her. For Rakove, and the hateful torture he had inflicted on Alim. For the boy, for obliging her to know that agony herself, and his violation of her innermost self.

The office's door chime made her jump.

She steadied herself and checked the feed of the external picter on one of the boxy imagifiers on her desk. A familiar face was illuminated by the reflected glare of the street-lumens. Melita thumbed a switch on the desk to deactivate the electromagnetic locks holding the heavy steel closed.

Edi Kamensk loomed in the doorway, his broad chest and shoulders made wider by a heavy synthleather coat and a thick woven jersey beneath it. Varangantua's wet season had thrown up one last squall before it gave way to the stifling heat of the dry months, and cold, wet air blew in around him to further upset the papers on her desk and floor.

He studied her warily. She hadn't told him what the psyker had done to her, but the former sanctioner had worked as Melita's bodyguard for four years. His look of mute concern had become all too familiar over the past few weeks as she stalked Rakove with single-minded zeal.

'What's wrong with your face?' Melita snapped.

Edi's expression dropped into its more typical, reassuring scowl. 'You ready?'

She was. After weeks of hunting, Rakove had finally been revealed to her. Tonight, she would expunge the debt of pain owed to Alim and lay to rest the ghost that haunted her. Melita was not a violent woman, but the visceral hate she had inherited from the psyker had only grown as she hounded his tormentor. Before the night was over, she would see Jorg Rakove delivered into the Valtteri's ungentle custody, or to the city's crematoria fields.

'Melita?' Edi prompted.

She looked down at Rakove's porcine glare and felt barbs pulling at the skin of her throat.

'Let's go.'

The twin beams of the groundcar's headlamps cut bright streaks through the pouring rain as they drove along deserted arterials and across pitch-black junctions. They had driven deep into the heart of the Spoil, following a route Edi and Melita knew well. Her business took them to every corner of the dilapidated sprawl, although it would have been foolish for either of them to let their familiarity turn into complacency.

'That's coming along,' said Edi as they crossed a span of elevated highway. The object of his comment was hard to miss. An expansive collection of rockcrete and brick buildings rose from a patch of derelict land half a mile to the south. The compound was lit by bright sodium lamps that shone in the darkness, illuminating dozens of men and women who were working despite the lateness of the hour.

In contrast to the districts surrounding the Spoil, construction was a major employer for the region's itinerant labourers.

So few basic utilities were available to the unfortunates that eked out their lives within the Spoil's borders, but every year a little more seemed to be added. In this case, the furnaces were intended to pipe power and heat into the nearby habs, although only for those who could pay for such a luxury.

'Sorokin wants it running before the end of the year.' Melita had been paying close attention to the erection of the furnaces. Every brick, bolt and cable was provided by Andreti Sorokin, the ganger-king of the Spoil. The city had abandoned the region to its squalor, and the Har Dhrol gangs had filled the void.

They drove on, leaving the builders to their task. The roads were almost empty, but that was typical. The Spoil's nightlife was a coy, tense affair. Those with the slate to spend freely were typically gangers, and were a liability to any revel house they frequented, as well as to anyone who happened to be sharing it with them. Most denizens of the Spoil kept to themselves after Alecto's wan sun had set, or else hid from their miseries in tiny drinking dens converted from the basement rooms of hab-blocks. Those found roaming the streets were usually stumbling to or from narco-pushers' corners.

But while venues for higher-class amusement were rare in the Spoil, they were not non-existent.

The Teseralde was a joy house, although like everything in the neglected morass of abandoned foundries and rotting hab-stacks of the Spoil, the revelry was a faded echo of what that title could mean in a true district of the city. Where a Dragosyl joy house might blaze with kaleidoscopic neon, the Teseralde's grime-hazed windows flickered with greasy yellow light, where they were not boarded up. Where Melita would have expected armour-clad private securitors standing sentinel over a carefully corralled queue of off-duty clerks and administrators, here gangers shook down the vagrants and dispossessed labourers who approached the entrance for proof they had sufficient slate for the night's amusements.

It wasn't even a purpose-built joy house. The Teseralde was set back from the street and had the look of a merchant-baron's townhouse. Three storeys of time- and toxin-etched stone reared above Melita as Edi steered their groundcar into the building's courtyard. Streams of chem-rich water fell from the mouths of gargoyles atop its eaves, and sculpted cherubim leered from the columned portico. The stone columns between which Edi and Melita drove would have once held iron gates to ensure the manse's occupants were undisturbed by the rabble, but the gates and the rest of the courtyard's railings had likely been wrested from their foundations and sold for the value of their metal by enterprising Spoilers long ago.

They were stopped just inside what remained of the joy house's boundary by a pair of gangers, who shone hand-lumens into the groundcar's interior. They glanced inside, then, evidently satisfied they were not a stub-gun-toting crew of rival gangers, pointed towards a covered depot.

Melita climbed out of the groundcar as soon as the engine died, bracing herself against the biting wind and torrential rain. Edi climbed out more slowly, one hand resting protectively on the vehicle's roof. He had not wanted to bring Katuschka, his prized antique Dymaxion Model 34, into the Spoil, fearing the jealousy of the gutter, but Melita had insisted. Everything that happened from this moment forward would be an exercise in projected status. In pretending at confidence and composure no matter what obstacles were set in her way.

She had dressed with that goal in mind. Though Melita

rarely made an effort at her attire, she had made her living as an info-broker for four years, and experience had taught her that appearances mattered on the street just as much as in the offices of a merchant-combine executor. Her expensive real-leather jacket, cut high above her hips, tight breeches and thick-soled calf-length boots were what she thought of as her armour. The face with which she met the world and its trials.

She hadn't brought Oriel, as much as she had wanted to. As much as she would have been reassured by the servo-skull's proximity, she knew that her quarry's paranoia would not permit her to bring so lethal an entity into his presence.

Edi rounded the groundcar's frame, shoulders hunched against the downpour, the hand-cannon at his hip visible beneath his coat. That would have to do.

They started for the joy house's portico, but a huddle of gangers in grey synthleathers loomed out of the shadows to bar their path.

'What you want, upclave?'

Melita didn't blink. 'I'm here to see the King.'

The lead ganger's facial tattoos contorted as he made a gesture of derision. 'You and half the scum of the Spoil. Piss off.'

'He'll want to see me.'

'Is that so?'

Melita dipped a hand inside her jacket and withdrew a blue slate. She held it between thumb and forefinger for a moment to ensure she had the ganger's attention.

'My name is Melita Voronova. He'll want to see me.'

She flicked the chip to the ganger, who smartly plucked it from the air. The bribe was on the high side for so small a thing as getting through the open door, but Melita reasoned that a flash of slate now would set the tenor for the conversation to come. Besides, it wasn't her money she was giving away.

The man sniffed, then stepped back to let Melita and Edi pass, but not before sending a member of his crew inside to warn of their arrival.

Heat billowed from the joy house's interior, foetid air steaming where it met the night's storm-blasted chill. The wet slap of humidity was foul, and Melita fought to keep her face neutral. It wasn't just the heat – the rain had blunted the Spoil's usual reek of refuse and open sewers, and so the ripe fug of compacted humanity was particularly sudden and repulsive.

They forced their way through the press of bodies, Melita leading but with Edi close behind. They passed from the vestibule into a larger reception hall, where the crowd thinned sufficiently for Melita to catch her breath.

The hall was dominated by a pair of staircases that curved from opposite walls up to the second level. The stairs formed an arch through which most of the crowd were trying to move, but the hall also branched left and right towards other, evidently less popular entertainments.

The joy house retained enough of its character as a former gilded manse to feel strangely dissonant. Vendors served pitchers of slatov from stalls set up beneath ornate coving. Bill papers advertising the joy house's diversions were pasted over discoloured patches of plastered wall that should have held portraits of the owner's kin. Men jostled one another in ill-tempered disagreement on a tiled floor that must have been the work of a dozen skilled artisans. An Imperial aquila carved from black marble crowned the apex of the arch under the stairs, a common affirmation of loyalty in the homes of the gilded. But in this house, the heads of both eagles had been hacked away, and the aquila's wings were similarly chipped back to nubs.

Melita couldn't see Edi's face, but she was sure he noticed the casual desecration of the Imperial emblem and was grateful that he kept his disapproval to himself. Despite accompanying her on almost all of her sojourns into the Spoil for the past four years, Edi had never lost his strangely innocent dismay at how far the sprawl and its denizens had fallen from the Emperor's light.

Both staircases were blocked by more knots of gangers clad in grey, who snarled at anyone that, either through curiosity or the accidental motion of the crowd, came too close. One man dressed more like a clerk than a street-blade stood halfway up the right-hand side, evidently waiting to catch Melita's eye. They pushed their way forward as he descended to meet them.

'I'm Nurem Babić.' He had to shout over the din of voices that suddenly roared from beneath the arch. 'This way.'

'Weapons first,' grunted one of the guards. Melita nodded in mute acceptance and held open the lapel of her coat to let the ganger reach in and withdraw her snub-nosed laspistol from its holster. Edi, with far less grace, gave up his enormous Sulymann Engager, his smaller backup autopistol and his jawsnapper. The last of these was handed over with particular reluctance – Melita was sure he carried the knuckleduster as a proxy for the shock maul he had worn for every day of his thirty-two years as a sanctioner.

They were led up the curve of the staircase and through a synthwood door. The cacophony of voices was reduced to a tolerable level for only a moment as Babić led them along a short corridor and opened the door at its end without knocking.

Many people claimed to rule areas of the Spoil. Even the lowest crew of street-blades could call a particular corner their territory. But, just like the rest of the city, true ownership was found much higher. A crew of narco-pushers might occupy a street, but a clave-captain controlled the block. And while the clave-captains might squabble amongst themselves, and even wage brief and bitter wars for particularly valuable tracts of land, they were all bound within the Har Dhrol, the alliance of gangs that had transformed the Spoil from a divided, catastrophically poor urban wilderness into a single, semi-coherent whole.

The man at the centre of that whole was Andreti Sorokin, the King of the Har Dhrol.

He bore a passing resemblance to Edi, in that they were both big men, powerfully built, but for whom time's knife had begun to cut. Sorokin's hair and beard were closely cropped, both more grey than black. He had a slightly hunched posture, but this emphasised rather than diminished the air of menace that bled from him. Sorokin was a hulking, ageing brawler who had built a throne for himself atop the bodies of every other Spoil ganger who had made the mistake of opposing his rise.

She knew from her informants within Sorokin's household that his eyesight was fading, but he wore no lens or other aids tonight. He stood as they entered, gesturing with a hand holding a glass of what looked like amasec to beckon them inside.

'Mistress Voronova, what an unexpected pleasure.'

Andreti Sorokin's voice was unlike any other. It started in the great barrel of his chest, deep as a grave, hoarse from a lifetime of whispered threats and bellowed curses. He spoke in a strangely wandering manner, lingering on some words and biting off others. It was deeply disconcerting, like almost everything about the King of the Har Dhrol.

'Messr Sorokin.'

'Andreti, please.'

Melita inclined her head. 'I was grateful for the invitation.'

Sorokin blinked, apparently nonplussed. 'Did I invite you, Mistress Voronova? Far as I see it, you have appeared suddenly before me, waving your masters' slate about, to interrupt a rare night of leisure.'

Melita registered his note of disapproval regarding her bribery of the doorman, but pressed on. 'You let it be known that you have Jorg Rakove. And that you'd be here tonight.'

'Yes, I did.' He abandoned his pretence immediately and waved a hand at one of the chairs that occupied the box. 'Well, come on then. Sit. Have a drink. Talk to me about Jorg Rakove.'

The fighting was a distraction Melita could have done without.

They sat in a pair of overstuffed armchairs at the edge of his private box, with Edi and Sorokin's own bodyguards standing near at hand. The box had evidently once been a balustraded landing overlooking one of the townhouse's receiving chambers. The enterprising operator of the occupied manse had sectioned off the landing into discrete spaces, like the private booths of a theatre, and Sorokin had occupied the largest of these, as was his right and privilege.

Beneath them was the fighting pit. The box overlooked the main hall, and at least three hundred people had crammed themselves into the narrow space. Whoever ran the joy house had prised up the flagstones at the hall's centre to create a shallow square, and this pit was hemmed in on all sides by a roaring crowd of gangers, labourers and other Spoil dregs.

Above them were more boxes, like Sorokin's, and from these more men and women cheered and jeered. The Spoil's makeshift joy houses and other venues of salacious entertainment were heady temptations for a certain class of gilded sensualist, drawn to the illicit substances and unlicensed flesh found at civilisation's edge. All of these were readily available in Setomir's and Dragosyl's own dens and alleys, but in the Spoil they were accompanied by the alien thrill of true poverty. Several knots of these gaudily dressed rakes occupied the boxes opposite Sorokin's, though they were outnumbered at least three to one by more sober companions – only the most foolhardy hedonist ventured beyond the Rustwater Canal without a sizeable contingent of their family's lifewards.

Melita watched as two men, stripped to the waist, emerged from the crowd and stepped down into the fighting pit. As odds were called and bets taken, Melita wondered how purposeful was Sorokin's choice of location for their meeting. Immediately, she dismissed the question as naive. Everything was a test.

A ringmaster was calling the fighters' names to roars of approbation, while another lifted a length of chain perhaps three yards long from the sand of the pit. With a surprising amount of ceremony, the ringmaster fixed each end of the chain to the fighters' wrists with a heavy metal cuff. Then he withdrew a pair of long-bladed knives from a case held by another assistant and spun them for the crowd's appreciation. With one final shout, he tossed the knives into opposite corners of the pit, and the fight was on.

Melita leant back as cries erupted from beneath her. Almost instantly, the tang of blood cut through the choking miasma of sweating humanity and noxiously sweet body scents.

Melita kept her face in an impassive mask and fought down the sensory bombardment.

'Where is he?'

Sorokin took a slow swallow of amasec before replying. 'Safe. Contained.'

'Rakove is scum,' she said between cheers. 'The Valtteri want him, and they'll pay to have him.' There was no point being coy. Both of them knew why they were there, and the rest was merely haggling over the cost.

'Before we get to that.' Sorokin leant back in the chair. He combined his odd mode of speech with a roaming, inconstant gaze, looking from the fighting pit to Melita to the crowd to his drink and back to the pit. 'What's a smart young thing like you doing in hock to that band of usurers and idolators?' His voice dropped low in his condemnation of the cartel.

Melita had assumed this would come up and had an answer ready. 'They pay well.'

'Is that right? Well, that is a shame.'

'How so?'

Sorokin's eyes stopped their roving and met hers. Melita felt the sudden force of his attention and judgement. His was a fierce, angry stare, a challenge to whatever or whomever he turned it on.

'We know each other of old. I thought better of you.'

She turned, uncertain how to take that. Melita and Sorokin had met perhaps three times in the past few years. Each encounter had been a moment of high tension for her, but Melita was surprised he remembered her at all.

She swiftly considered how best to respond to his apparent disappointment. 'You don't seem to mind being seen to deal with the Valtteri.'

That was a risky play. It was common knowledge that Sorokin, the warlord who had built an empire from the ashes of the Spoil, was backed by the Valtteri Cartel. He had reined in the excesses of his clave-captains, outlawed the engine-gangers that preyed on Valtteri convoys, and in return they kept him in power, with a steady flow of slate, weapons and whatever else he desired. Or, at least, that was the rumour that had become the truth on the street.

Melita saw that her jibe had landed. 'Dealing's one thing. Being at the end of their leash is another. I'm beholden to nothing and no one. I don't think you can say the same.'

They sat in silence, or the closest thing to silence with howls of glee and derision heaving up from the pit.

'So, why is it your *employers*' – he put a special emphasis on the word – 'want him?'

Melita was relieved to be back on easier ground. 'What has Rakove told you?'

'Told me? I haven't spoken to him. The bastard doesn't even know that I'm the one who has him. He thinks he's holed up in a safehouse used by a bunch of bliss-pushers.'

That was a lot of information to give away, and Melita wondered how much of it was true. In a place as vast as the Spoil, it would be almost impossible to narrow down a list of locations that narco-pushers might use to stash their goods.

'You didn't answer me,' growled Sorokin. 'What's Rakove to the Valtteri?'

Melita had gone back and forth on just how much truth to give him. 'He harboured a psyker. Inside the Spoil. Used it to attack the cartel's interests.'

Sorokin made a face, a pious scowl at the mention of heretic witchery, but Melita could see that he had already known everything she had told him.

Another gale of hoots and whistles erupted from the fighting pit. Sorokin gestured over the balcony's edge. 'Who'd you favour, hmm?' he asked, suddenly switching topics.

'I'm sorry?'

'Let's say I give you the mutant-hoarding scum if you pick the winner.'

Melita scoffed. 'You're not going to do that.'

'I might.' He stared back at her. Insincere though the offer clearly was, his challenge was very real. She frowned and leant forward to look over the balustrade's lip.

The two new fighters could not have been more different. One was a mountain of a man, his upper body one vast slab of scarred muscle. He looked like a foundry worker, or perhaps a stevedore for the shallow-bottomed hulks that crossed the Rustwater with cheaply made goods turned out from the Spoil's workshops.

The other was a woman, also tall but surely no more than a third of the man's weight. She wore a cut-down bodyglove, exposing lithely muscled arms. Her hair was shaved to a finger's width all over, and she spun her knife with rapid flicks of her wrist, watching for her opponent's reaction.

Despite herself, Melita tried to gauge which would be the victor. The crowd evidently favoured the woman, cheering at each flash of her knife, jeering the giant's caution as he turned in the centre of the pit, moving as quickly as he could to follow the woman's dancing motion. In less than a minute, both of them were bleeding from thin cuts and off-hand blows. Melita winced. The pain from those wounds must have been immense, tugged and jarred as they were by the demands of the fight.

The woman changed direction with an elegant spin, but the man read the move and was ready with a clenched fist swung backhanded. She rolled away from the blow, but only as far as the chain that bound them together would allow.

He started to heave. The woman's heels left trails in the blood-wet sand as she resisted, strength set against strength. But then she darted in, left hand rising quickly to twitch the sudden slack in the chain. The curl of metal leapt up, but at the last second the man jerked his head away so that the chain lashed across his temple, rather than blinding him as the woman had intended.

She was on him in a heartbeat, blade moving like quicksilver as the giant backpedalled. She caught him three times with shallow cuts to his massive torso, but the man's roars of pain made her overconfident. As she stepped in for the kill, he checked his backward motion. She ran straight into his hugely muscled hip, staggered away, and in the brief second of confusion the giant reached forward, almost casually, and dragged the length of his blade across her bicep.

The woman reeled back, blade abandoned so she could clutch at the horrendous wound that had laid her arm open to the bone. The crowd groaned as the giant raised his hands in triumph. The motion jerked the woman's hand from her mutilated arm, and blood sprayed in an arc into the faces of the front rank of the crowd. Melita lurched back, sick to her stomach.

Sorokin half stood from his seat. 'Nicely done!' The mob roared back, their bias towards the stricken woman forgotten in the face of Sorokin's approval. The victor, for his part, tapped the flat of his wet knife against his chest in salute, then waited for the ringmaster to remove the chain from his wrist. The woman's crew had already freed her and were pushing their way to the opposite side of the hall.

He settled back into his seat. 'Well, too slow there. Shame, too. It's in no one's interests to have a man like Rakove walking the street.'

Melita's pulse quickened. She was almost certain that he was teasing her, looking for another angle from which to test and probe her. But the fear of losing Rakove when she was so close was palpable.

'It is a shame.' Melita managed to keep her voice level. 'Since I'd have picked him.'

'Easy to say so now.' Sorokin's eyes glittered with amusement, glad that Melita was keeping up with his game. 'But, for argument's sake, why?'

'"You can be quick and you can be canny, but being tough enough to ride the blows is what sees you through a fight."' That had been one of her mother's pearls of wisdom, hard learnt from a life spent warring with other smuggling clans beneath the massive stanchions of the Dragosyl voidports.

'Is that so?' Sorokin seemed to ponder her words. 'So you'd always bet on the big man?'

'Usually.' Melita had a premonition of approaching horror but was powerless to stop it.

'Right, then. I have a new proposal. You can have Rakove if your man wins a bout in the pit on your behalf.'

Melita froze. Behind her, she felt Edi stiffen.

'I mean it.' The mockery was gone, or at least it had disappeared behind a mask of rigid intensity. 'Blood for blood, the way everything is settled out here beyond the world's edge.'

Melita's heart pounded, loud enough to hear. She was paralysed. She had been so clear that Sorokin had come intending to make a deal, but his careless jibes and goading had thrown her off balance.

'I...' She trailed off. She would never allow Edi to set foot in the pit, but she could not let Rakove evade her revenge. 'There's no way you'll–'

Edi twitched the coat from his shoulders. 'I'll need to borrow one of those knives.'

She spun in her seat. 'Edi, don't.'

As soon as she said the words, an involuntary whisper, something changed in Sorokin's eyes. Triumph. He'd got what he was looking for. He'd cut through her layers of front and indifference and forced her to let slip something real, something true about herself.

Melita cared about Edi. He was probably the only person left in Varangantua who still mattered to her, and Sorokin had effortlessly drawn her into giving that vulnerability away.

'Maybe there's no need,' said Sorokin, leaning back. 'After all, folk are lining up to fight in front of me. I wouldn't like to deprive some young talent their turn in the spotlight.'

Melita seethed. She had lost all patience with Sorokin's antics, his casual jests and jibes. 'You didn't come here to gamble. You're holding Rakove because you're looking to get paid. What's your price?'

His eyes narrowed, either with amusement at her temper or anger at her insinuation. 'Make me an offer.'

The cartel's agents had given her close to a free hand to obtain Rakove's head. She could offer him the deeds to land and property in half the city, off-world treasures, immunity for his agents and allies beyond the Spoil or enough slate to bury anything that could still trouble him. But Melita's blood was still up, and she gave into a reckless impulse.

'Rejuvenat chems.'

Sorokin's stare turned brittle, just slightly, enough to know that she had struck a nerve in return.

The King of the Har Dhrol was an old man in a world that

punished weakness. For the gilded, age was nothing but a number, their careless immortality bought with the labour of the millions who toiled at their command. Sorokin was undoubtedly as rich as any three merchant-barons Melita could name, but the Spoil was not the place to find the exclusive, highly secured therapeutic clinics one needed to enter in order to achieve rejuvenat's full results.

He gave a rough sort of laugh, a recognition of a point landed. 'Nice try, but no. Those I can source myself, if I were ever to be so vain as to want them.'

'Then what?'

Sorokin said nothing for a long time. Then he slowly stood, all of a sudden wearing the years that Melita had mocked. He rounded his armchair, ignoring the cries for his attention from the pit below, and crossed the box to a narrow shelf that held an array of glass bottles.

'I am constantly disappointed by you upclavers' low regard for what I have done. What I'm trying to do.' He lifted a bulb-like decanter of amasec and poured himself a tall measure. 'Don't get me wrong, I understand it. Everyone needs somebody to look down on. But it does… irk me.'

Realisation dawned. In the thirty years since Sorokin had risen to command the length and breadth of the Spoil, he hadn't merely exploited the people still trapped inside it. He had built. Cut off from the city's infrastructure, Sorokin had set about creating his own, like the furnaces she and Edi had passed on their way to the Teseralde. For all that the Spoil's facade was broken and its bones rotten, Sorokin was doing what he could to graft, piece by piece, the muscle and sinew of a functioning district onto the Spoil's decaying frame.

But there would be so much beyond his reach. Bricks and

mortar were one thing, but to build generatoria, sanitation plants, data-junctions – that required complex equipment and refined parts, machined to the exacting templates of the Adeptus Mechanicus. Such things would be difficult to acquire in the quantities that the Spoil needed, even for the King of the Har Dhrol.

She spoke slowly and carefully. 'I'm certain that the produce of the Valtteri's manufactoria can be made available to you, Messr Sorokin.'

He turned, glass half raised to his lips. He grinned. 'Not bad. I had to walk you right up to it, but not bad.'

Sorokin made a summoning gesture with his free hand. Babić, the ganger who had led them in, crossed the box quickly and handed him a pasteboard card. Melita could see the tight alphanumerics of a loc-ref stamped onto one side, and nothing else. She fought the desperate temptation to try and snatch it from the old man's hands. Sorokin flicked the card with a thick finger.

'I'll have Babić send you a list. If everything on it – and I mean everything, to the last bolt and rivet – is delivered to my crews by midnight tomorrow, then I'll see to it that Rakove will be here the following morning.'

'You'll have it.' She made the promise instantly, carelessly.

'Mess me around and he'll vanish beyond even your powers to dredge up.'

'They won't.'

Sorokin, conscious of her stare, continued to toy with the card. 'What's Rakove to you, Mistress Voronova?'

Melita tried to affect nonchalance, although it was far too late for that. 'Do you care?'

Sorokin drew out the silence for several rapid beats of Melita's heart, then shrugged. 'I suppose not.' The ganglord tossed the loc-ref to her like a card sharp, and Melita plucked it from the air. She had him.

Melita caught the tremor in her hand as it started, but too late to stop the surge of sensation that overtook her.

The control stave for the agony collar was in Rakove's pocket. She was inside his mind, and she could feel the bulge of the stave against her hip. The hatred polluting his thoughts was a bitter heat, a fever that set her limbs trembling as much as the collar's barbs. There was nothing about her that he considered human, no shred of pity or guilt for the torment he inflicted. What pity he had was for himself, forced to taint his soul by proximity to her abhuman existence.

She tensed, mewling pleas rising to her lips, as he withdrew the stave and thumbed it on.

Sorokin was still talking. 'I have four men keeping an eye on him. Don't kill any of them.'

Melita breathed out, trying to control the violent shivering in her chest. She sensed Edi place a hand against the armchair's back, as close as he dared to a comforting grip. Melita leant away from him and instead pressed a thumb against the edge of the card.

Rakove had lost. She had freed Alim, and now she would trap him in his own cage. She would show him where the limits of *her* mercy lay.

If Sorokin noticed her distraction, he didn't comment on it. 'Do you know why I'm giving Rakove to you? Other than the fact that he brought a witch onto my ground, and I won't harbour any man who trifles with their kind.'

It took her a moment to stammer a reply. 'Why?' Melita itched to leave, to escape the stink of blood and sweat and the changeable warlord whose word was law.

'Because you asked.' He drained his glass, placed it on the table between them and flicked it onto its side, where it rolled back and forth. 'I let you learn I had him, but you'd have found out eventually. You're a smart one.'

Melita was still too caught up in the aftermath of the memory to register his compliment.

'But you came here to ask me for him. I like that. It shows respect. Shows we understand one another.'

The old man picked up his glass, turning it one way and another in the greasy light. 'But, on the other hand, the Valtteri sent you. Not that any of the top men would ever come here themselves – I've made my peace with that. But they have an army of faceless worms to fetch and carry for them, and yet they sent you. Why'd you think that is?'

Melita knew exactly why, and it had nothing to do with Sorokin. It had been a test. The cartel had adopted her into their organisation because she'd been the one to find Alim when every other organ of their will had failed, and because she had been desperate enough to sell her skills to them.

The test hadn't been to track Rakove down – her masters had been entirely confident that she was capable of that. No, the true test had been this night, in whether she could acquire him and for what price. They had given her a free hand to spend as she had to because their coffers were that deep and their wroth that great, but she would be judged on what she had given away in return. It was impossible to know how well she had done by that metric – she was sure that Sorokin's list of demands would represent an extortionate price for the sale of one man.

Sorokin needed to hear none of this. She forced a smile. 'Because they knew you'd like me, Messr Sorokin.'

He laughed at that, with a sound like a canid's bark. 'That could be it, right enough.'

He lifted the decanter and poured himself another measure. 'Go on then, clear off with your prize. Let me see if I can't salvage something from this evening.'

Melita stood, grateful to be away, still shaken by the flash of memory and the fear of almost losing Edi to the pit.

She clutched the card in her hand. She had stumbled at almost every hurdle Sorokin had placed in her path. She was leaving with what she had come for only because he had wanted to give it away. She had failed by almost every measure, except the one that mattered.

Sorokin rapped his glass against the decanter's side to stop her as she reached the door. 'Good to see you, Mistress Voronova. Until next you need something.'

Melita said nothing, and slipped out of the box.

The previous day's storm had not abated, and the sound of freezing rain breaking against the groundcar's bodywork was the only sound in Melita's world.

She and Edi sat inside Katuschka's carefully maintained interior, two blocks from the loc-ref Sorokin had provided. The Valtteri had moved quickly, marshalling their considerable resources to meet Sorokin's price. A well-guarded convoy had rumbled across the Rustwater Canal a few hours earlier, loaded with the future of the Spoil's hesitant restoration.

Now, all that was left was to collect what they had bought.

Her vambrace pinged as Oriel registered the Valtteri's approach. She was wearing the lattice, her home-made rig for transporting the guardian servo-skull. The chromed skull squatted on her shoulder, its needler lurking at the corner of her sight, its suite of sensors feeding information to the curved data-slate that was clamped around her forearm.

They came in two of their enormous Shiiv Hegemons, each closer in size to an enforcer riot-wagon than a civilian groundcar. Their huge flanks showed the insignia of the Reisiger Company, a band of mercenaries who handled much of the cartel's security and related activities.

Melita and Edi had no role in what was to come, but there had never been any question that she would be there for Rakove's capture.

The two Hegemons came to a stop at the end of the street, surprisingly quiet for vehicles of such size. The rear of one of the groundcars opened and a quartet of mercenaries emerged. With professional efficiency, they trotted towards the hab-block's door, which was opened for them by an unseen figure within. They disappeared inside.

The seconds ticked by, agonisingly slowly.

Melita couldn't sit idle. She opened the groundcar's door and leant out, and the servo-skull detached from the lattice with a purr of its suspensors. With a flurry of tapped commands, she sent the skull up into the darkness, pursuing the mercenaries who had begun their climb through the levels of the hab-block, raindrops rolling from its silver plating.

Watching through the skull's thermal sensor on her vambrace, Melita could follow the progress of the Valtteri men as they rose through the hab-block's stairwell. Other smears of colour showed residents retreating into their rooms, no doubt fearing the sudden tramp of heavy bootsteps outside their habs.

Melita panned up. The first of the Valtteri men had reached the third floor, and they were evidently stacking up outside the target hab. Inside were a clutch of figures, but Melita had no way of knowing which was Rakove. They were evidently sitting in the hab's communal area. She made a note to try to speak to the gangers who had been Rakove's minders – anything he might have told them could be relevant to tracing his elusive backer.

One of the shapes twitched around, its limbs a smear of colour as it stood. There was just enough time for dread to settle in Melita's stomach, and then gunfire shattered the night.

Melita's head rose on instinct towards the sound, in the same moment that Edi pressed her protectively down into her seat. She struggled under his weight, desperate to know what was happening.

More shots rang out. The harsh bark of a large-calibre stub pistol and the chatter of autoguns. She awkwardly twisted her body to bring her vambrace up in front of her and refocused the imagifier. Melita switched from the thermal sensor to Oriel's picter, but the skull saw nothing but the flash of multiple muzzle flares.

'Fuck!'

She pulled herself from beneath Edi's weight and pushed open the groundcar's door. She leapt out and raced the length of the block. She rounded the corner, almost falling on the slick, broken paving.

The mercenaries were emerging from the hab-block, surrounded by others who had appeared from the Hegemon's passenger compartments. Slung between two of the armoured bodies was a heavy-set figure, knees scraping on the steps, head slumped forward to almost touch the rockcrete.

Melita ran on, reaching for the laspistol holstered beneath her shoulder. She struggled to clear it from the synthleather, swore as she stumbled, and then stopped short as one of the mercenaries stepped into her path.

'Out of the way!' All rational thought had fled with the first gunshot. The Valtteri's need for what Rakove knew had ceased to matter, if it ever had to her. Melita would kill him, here and now. For Alim, for herself. For all his crimes, against her and whomever else Rakove had wronged in his brutal life.

But he was already dead.

The mercenaries laid Rakove on the street, blood flowing into the puddles of acrid rainwater.

Melita gaped, thoughts misfiring to the rapid tempo of wasted adrenaline. 'What the hells happened?'

The mercenaries ignored her, busying themselves with unloading their guns and pulling off their armour. They seemed far from happy – one of them would have to explain to the Valtteri's executors how they had so catastrophically failed at what should have been the simple collection of an unarmed man. But first they would have to explain it to her.

'Well?'

One of the Reisiger men stopped peeling the sections of plate from his chest. 'The target grabbed the weapon of one of the gangers that were with him. We had to drop him.'

An overwhelming weight settled on her shoulders. She'd hoped to feel a measure of relief, but all she felt was frustration. The Valtteri's questions would go unanswered – whoever had supported Rakove's operation would evade their grasp and perhaps make use of some other unfortunate to try again. Alim's torturer was dead, but justice would have seen him suffer as Melita knew the boy had suffered. A quick death was not revenge enough for her.

'By the damned Throne!' Melita tore the data-slate from her arm and hammered it into the asphalt. Shards of plex and arcane electronics flew away into the darkness. The mercenary turned back to the Hegemon's interior, ignoring Melita's outburst.

She suddenly became aware of Edi's grip on her shoulder, pulling her away. Melita shrugged him off and turned, choosing Edi to be the target of her frustrated rage and confusion.

'Why were you going to fight last night? Back at the joy house?' She'd been holding in the question for the entire day, but now it erupted unbidden. The former sanctioner said nothing.

'Answer me.'

'Because you needed this,' he said finally. He turned to look at her, face streaked with rain. Melita felt oddly alarmed by the strength of feeling that filled his eyes.

'Whatever that witch did to you...' Edi looked like he wanted to spit, but instead he silently made the sign of the aquila over his chest. 'Whatever it did, it got inside your head. I've watched you. You always work like you're possessed, but these past months you've been manic. Hyper-focused, like only one thing existed. You needed to see this done, and I wanted to help you do it.'

Melita gaped. Without a word spoken between them on the subject for two months, Edi had cut to the core of her turmoil. She felt exposed, laid bare just as she had been by Alim's casual penetration of her mind.

He was right, of course. It might not have been the catharsis she had hoped for, but she had needed to see Rakove broken, one way or another. She glanced back to watch the Valtteri men load the body into one of their vehicles.

'What do you want to do now?' Edi asked.

Melita sighed. She knew it was too much to hope that she would be rid of Alim's implanted memories. They were a part of her now, a parallel life of trauma and fear that she would have to endure, just as the psyker had. But perhaps, if she was lucky, she might finally have a night of unbroken rest.

'Take me home.'

YOUR NEXT READ

BLOODLINES
by Chris Wraight

An investigation into a missing member of a wealthy family leads Probator Agusto Zidarov into a web of lies and danger amidst the criminal cartels of Varangantua. As the net closes in, Zidarov falls further into darkness from which he may never return…

ABOUT THE AUTHORS

Jonathan D Beer is a science fiction and alternative history writer. Equally obsessed with the 19th century and the 41st millennium, he lives with his wife and assorted cats in the untamed wilderness of Edinburgh, Scotland. His Warhammer Crime stories include 'Old Instincts', 'Service' and 'Chains', and the novel *The King of the Spoil.*

Mike Brooks is a science fiction and fantasy author who lives in Nottingham, UK. His work for Black Library includes the Horus Heresy Primarchs novel *Alpharius: Head of the Hydra,* the Warhammer 40,000 novels *Rites of Passage, Warboss* and *Brutal Kunnin,* the Necromunda novel *Road to Redemption* and the novellas *Wanted: Dead* and *Da Gobbo's Revenge.* When not writing, he plays guitar and sings in a punk band, and DJs wherever anyone will tolerate him.

Gary Kloster is a writer, a stay-at-home father, a librarian and a martial artist – sometimes all in the same day, seldom all at the same time. His work for Black Library includes the Age of Sigmar novel *The Last Volari,* the Necromunda novella *Spark of Revolution,* and a number of short stories. He lives among the corn in the American Midwest.

Jude Reid lives in Glasgow with her husband and two daughters, and writes in the narrow gaps between full-time work as a surgeon, wrangling her kids and failing to tire out a border collie. In what little free time she has, she enjoys tabletop roleplaying, ITF Tae Kwon Do and inadvisably climbing big hills. Her many stories for Black Library include the Warhammer 40,000 novel *Creed: Ashes of Cadia*.

Chris Thursten is a writer and video game developer from Bath, UK. His stories for Black Library include 'Cauldron of Blood' and 'Pain Engine'.

YOUR NEXT READ

LEVIATHAN
by Darius Hinks

A decorated lieutenant of the Ultramarines recognises the signs of an imminent tyranid attack, and launches a desperate counter-offensive to save Regium, a proud Imperial world.

An extract from
Leviathan
by Darius Hinks

The tacticarium had been carved from burial chambers – chiselled from catacombs that snaked beneath the city. Auspex shrines and cogitators now obscured most of the walls, but in a few places fragments of sacred art were still visible. It mostly showed tree-roots, snaking down from the world's surface and encasing its core, cradling it in a nest of tendrils. But the more recent additions depicted the Emperor, His sword trailing leaves rather than flames and His helmet sporting a crown of knotted branches.

The chamber, once a site of prayer and sacrifice, was now full of quiet industry and the cold flicker of viewscreens. Helots and comms officers were hunched over runeboards, dressed in smartly pressed uniforms rather than priestly robes. Mind-scrubbed servitors scuttled spider-like over logic engines, their faces grey and toothless and their limbs replaced with bionics.

Lieutenant Varus Castamon of the Ultramarines First Company was aware of the chamber's history, but his attention was focused entirely on the present. He watched parchment spooling from one of the servitors, then carefully tore some off, processing the information with inhuman speed. The symbols conjured images of warships in his mind, behemoths knifing through the void towards the outermost reaches of the system, weapons batteries coming online. He thought of his brothers, tracing their fingers over strips of vellum fixed to their armour, reciting blood-sworn oaths. The thought quickened his pulse and he wished, more than anything, that he was with them on this mission.

Across from him, Brother-Librarian Zuthis Abarim stood at the centre of the room, watching images projected from a domed holo-table, while a third Ultramarine, Brother-Sergeant Tanaro, was standing nearer to Castamon. Scattered around the rest of the room, dwarfed by the three Ultramarines, were dozens of humans – senior Militarum officers and their aides, all wearing starched regimental finery. Further back, scurrying through the shadows, making adjustments to the stacks of logic engines, were red-robed adepts of the Adeptus Mechanicus.

'How long?' asked Castamon, dropping the parchment.

'The strike force is approaching the edge of the system now, my lord,' said a helot, staring at a viewscreen. 'The deep-void returns are faint, but we can just about place the ships.' He pointed out a cluster of faint dots hanging over the holo-table. 'They'll shortly be passing the moons of Krassus.'

Castamon gestured for the Militarum officers to come closer. They obeyed his silent command, some trying to catch his eye but most trying to avoid it. He tried to imagine how they saw him. As a monster, probably. He was huge, of course, like any Space Marine, three heads taller than a man. His skin was dark and weathered and his head was shaved, displaying three scars that raked down over his skull – fat, silvery gouges left by a predator's claw. His blocky jaw was edged with a short silver beard, and his eyes were set deep under an anvil-hard brow. He did not seek to intimidate, but he was comfortable with the fact that he did. There were few who could hold his gaze for long.

He recognised all of the officers and they would have been surprised to know how well he knew the details of their military careers. Castamon was a warrior. He had no interest in politics, least of all the human variety. But he approached his posting on Regium with the same rationality and diligence he applied to everything else, remembering the words of his Lord Commander. *Fortify your mind with study. Prepare for all outcomes.* As he scrutinised the faces, he recalled facts gleaned from data crystals and genealogical tracts. Rather than soldiers he saw allegiances and rivalries, flaws and obsessions, debts and hopes – every shade of human frailty. They looked proud and determined, trying to hide how nervous they felt in his presence. They were good people. Whatever their failings, they had endured. They had survived long enough to see silver in their beards and feel aches in their bones. They were the exceptional few.

+The next couple of days will test them.+

The words formed telepathically in Castamon's mind. There was a time when he would have found the experience distasteful, repulsive even, but the voice was familiar now, the voice of a friend. He looked over at Abarim. The Librarian's suit of battleplate was even larger and more impressive than Castamon's. His head was buried in a thick ceramite cowl and his armour was intricately inscribed, covered with runes and horned-skull designs. He stood statuelike, towering over the humans. The lower half of his face was hidden behind a rebreather, but his eyes were visible and they shone fiercely as they focused on Castamon. He was gripping a force axe larger than any of the humans, a magnificent relic, worked with the same runic designs as his armour and shimmering with the same light that spilled from his eyes. Castamon noticed, with faint amusement, that none of the Militarum officers were standing near him.

This should not take days, he thought. *The ships are closing in on Krassus.*

+Tyrus has yet to locate his prey. And while he hunts, discontent spreads. You saw the crowds outside. They are scared. And scared people make dangerous decisions. Governor Seroc is too tolerant.+

You know my thoughts on the matter. Seroc is a good man. These people can police their own homes.

+You confuse lambs with wolves. Seroc is not equal to the task. None of them are.+

They need answers, that is all.

+Answers only beg more questions.+

Abarim would not usually address him in such an abrupt manner. He sounded almost bitter. The Librarian had been in pain for over a week and, though Abarim would never admit it, Castamon suspected his pain was growing worse. Pain was rarely a consideration for an Adeptus Astartes warrior, but Castamon knew this was not a physical suffering. It was something beyond his understanding – something linked to Abarim's esoteric skills. He needed to pursue the matter, but this was not the time. He wanted the soldiers out of his command bunker as quickly as possible.

He looked around the room. 'Governor Seroc asked me to speak to you, but I will keep this brief. We all know why we are here. There is panic and hysteria on Regium. Nightmares are spilling into people's waking hours. And there is a resurgence of the separatist threat, despite our labours in the spring. The separatists have a new creed, preaching of cataclysms and supernatural beings. But let me tell you this: there will be no cataclysm. There are no such supernatural beings. And the separatists are merely opportunists, seeking to regain a vestige of their former power. The cause of the nightmares is biological, not spiritual. It can be measured, combated and reversed. This planetwide hysteria stems from a foe that my battle-brothers and I have encountered before.'

'People want to know why the Ultramarines are leaving Regium,' said one of the officers, his tone brittle. 'That's one of the main catalysts of this current panic. Perhaps if we'd briefed people beforehand we could have allayed their fears.'

Castamon looked down at the man. 'We are briefing people *now.*' He pointed to the planet hovering in the air near Abarim, drawing their attention to a swirl of red light that was approaching it. 'The anomaly you see near Krassus is not a natural phenomenon. Nor is it a warp storm. It is the remnants of a xenos fleet.'

Some of the officers frowned as they studied the shapes, while others whispered to their aides.

'It is a fragment of an alien armada known as Hive Fleet Leviathan,' Castamon continued. 'It was first spotted several months ago, fleeing past the orbital shipyards of Hydraphur in the galactic north. The warships of the Navis Imperialis dealt with some of the aliens, but a few stragglers survived and fled south. We can only surmise what drove them this way, to the west. Perhaps they were savaged by another xenos fleet. Or by void-dwelling predators. Perhaps they were scattered many years ago by the emergence of the Great Rift. We may never know. But a few survivors are now skirting the outermost borders of this system.'

Some of the officers shifted position and others cleared their throats, about to ask questions, but Castamon raised his hand for silence.

'The creatures belong to a recognised xenotype. The Great Devourer. *Tyranids.* Little is known of their origins, but our Chapter has waged war against them in other systems and I can tell you this: they have no connection to the forces seeking to overthrow the Emperor. The heretics who attacked us in the spring sought to breach the Sanctus Line because they wish to invade the Sol System. They sought a route to Terra. But the tyranids are different. They are driven only by senseless hunger. A strategic defensive measure such as the Sanctus Line is beyond their comprehension. Everything we know about them indicates that they are a species of purely bestial predators. They have no inkling of this planet's tactical importance. However…' He paused. 'As they skirt the edge of this system, they *will* be drawn to Krassus.' He nodded to the planet at the edge of the system. 'A vast world, rich in biomass. A place where they could feed and reproduce. My Apothecary Biologis, an expert in the dark matter of xenos, believes they will be unable to resist it.'

He paused, looking round the room again, pleased to see the concentration on people's faces. 'Which presents us with an opportunity we cannot ignore. These abhorrent xenos cannot be allowed to taint our border with Segmentum Solar and, thanks to Krassus, we have a chance to stop them. We can prevent them advancing any further from the Galactic West. Krassus will be like a beacon to them. Their attention will be focused *entirely* on it. So, they will be slow to notice this.'

He pointed to another shape in the hololith – a cluster of blinking white arrowheads, heading towards Krassus. 'At this very moment, my battle-brother Lieutenant Tyrus is leading a strike force to cut this canker from the void. I have assured my superiors that these stragglers will come no closer to Holy Terra. Tyrus is a warrior of great renown and he is accompanied by *two-thirds* of the Ultramarines stationed here on Regium.'

An elderly officer spoke up. 'Which is exactly why people are panicking, my lord. Sending the majority of your Ultramarines off-world seems reckless. What if heretics attack us from the void again? The Sanctus Line is always a target. That's why you're here. If heretics know we've lost so many of our Ultramarines, they'll see a chance to attack.'

Castamon nodded. 'The same concern was voiced by Governor Seroc. My original plan was to lead my entire force to Krassus. But, as you have observed, Regium is always a potential target. So, after much thought, I decided to remain here with a third of my garrison. If there are any more acts of piracy or orbital strikes, we shall have no difficulty dealing with them. Strike Force Krassus will be heading back within a matter of days. The tyranids will be eliminated quickly and the full garrison will be restored here. I have assured Governor Seroc there will not be a prolonged engagement at the edge of the system.'

The elderly officer shook his head. 'You were deployed here to protect Regium. And, as you said yourself, the aliens out near Krassus are few in number. Why did you have to send so many men?'

'Why did you have to send *any* men?' asked another officer. 'Why not report the matter so it could be dealt with by someone else? From what you describe, the xenos threat is insignificant.'

'Insignificant?' Some of the soldiers paled as they heard

the warning in Castamon's tone. 'You betray your ignorance.' Images of bloodshed filled his mind. 'I have seen worlds devoured by a single tyranid swarm. They do not threaten. They do not bargain. They have no interest in wealth or power. We are naught to them but meat. If I allow them to leave this system, they will spawn. They will thrive. And they will consume.'

His words were followed by a troubled silence. Then one of the officers spoke up, his expression rigid as he battled to meet Castamon's gaze. 'Governor Seroc sent us here to discuss the rioting and insurrection, but also the dreams and the madness. What does that have to do with aliens at the edge of the system?'

Castamon was impressed by the man's nerve, but he replied in a tone that made it clear this was a briefing, not a debate. 'My Apothecary Biologis has theorised that the tyranids are behind this psychosis. There is much he cannot explain, but his underlying logic is sound. I have *seen* this happen before. Whether it is intentional or not, the presence of tyranids in a system induces hysteria.'

The man looked incredulous. 'People are burning down manufactories because of something that's happening on the other side of the system?'

'People are burning manufactories because, even from here, even from light years away, they feel the hunger of the Great Devourer.' Castamon looked at the red lights, pulsing blood-like above the table. 'They are unfathomable. They are your nightmares given form.' He waved at the V-shaped group of arrowheads. 'And we will grind them under our heel.'